BLUEBEARD

Operation Bluebeard will be the biggest snatch in history. A top KGB official, persuaded to defect, is to be plucked off a Russian cruise ship at a Spanish port. 'Bluebeard', however, knows too many embarrassing details about moles in British Intelligence, and MI6 are determined to get to him first, when the ship calls at Marseilles. Who better to accomplish this tricky, outrageous task than the elite SBS Team Alpha? Making their way secretly through French waterways, they come under vicious attack, betrayed from the start. Things will get even tougher when they reach Marseilles – and Bluebeard himself.

BLUEBEARD

BLUEBEARD

by

John Kerrigan

Magna Large Print Books
Long Preston, North Yorkshire,
BD23 4ND, England.

British Library Cataloguing in Publication Data.

Kerrigan, John
    Bluebeard.

    A catalogue record of this book is
    available from the British Library

    ISBN   0-7505-1910-X

First published in Great Britain 1984
by Century Publishing Co. Ltd.

Copyright © John Kerrigan 1984

Cover illustration © Len Thurston by arrangement with
P.W.A. International Ltd.

The moral right of the author has been asserted

Published in Large Print 2003 by arrangement with
Eskdale Publishing

Magna Large Print is an imprint of Library Magna Books Ltd.

Printed and bound in Great Britain by
T.J. (International) Ltd., Cornwall, PL28 8RW

Bluebeard: A fairy-tale character: a man who marries and kills one wife after another.

Webster's Dictionary

BOOK ONE

A Mission Is Proposed

'Ye have scarce the soul of a louse,' he said,
'but the roots of sin are there.'

Rudyard Kipling

1

'Benbulbin ... Truskmore ... Ben Weskin,' the Number One said, pointing out the peaks on the 'periphot'* as all around him the ratings tensed over their green-glowing instruments. They were still outside Irish territorial waters, but the men of Her Majesty's Submarine *Daring* knew it was vital to their mission not to be spotted, even by a passing fishing boat.

'Classiehawn Castle,' the Number One continued, tapping the photograph with his pencil, 'with here, Mullaghmore harbour. A typical holiday village complex, as you can see, gentlemen.'

The men of the SBS's élite Alpha Team craned their heads to get a better glimpse of the harbour which would be their starting point.

'Looks quite busy, Commander,' drawled Lieutenant Mallory, their leader, in that

*A panoramic shot taken through a submarine's periscope

11

casual, cool, upper-class way of his.

'To be expected, Mallory, at this time of the year, you know,' the Number One replied. As he spoke he stared wonderingly at Mallory's harshly handsome face and blue cynical eyes. It was hard to believe that this young Marine officer had been first to land on the Falklands and had later gone on to snatch a top-secret weapon right from under the noses of the Reds. He looked as if he would be more at home in Clubland, squiring expensive popsies to expensive West End night spots and getting himself written up in the gossip column of the *Daily Mail* as a 'well-known man about town'. 'August is after all the most popular holiday time, even in the Republic. These days the Irish take as many holidays as the, er ... Brits,' he said, with a faint grin on his pale submariner's face.

'Irish gits!' rasped Sergeant David Ross in his harsh Gorbals voice, face flushed and angry as always. 'The only good thing about them is that they banjo a lot o' each other.'

'Lot o' banjo in Ireland of North,' agreed Corporal Bin Bahadur of the Gurkhas in his strange, fractured English. As usual, there was a grin on his slant-eyed, glistening face at the thought of action. 'Pity no Gurkha

12

there. He banjo good.'

'I was dating a bint from Ireland once,' began Marine Will Rogers, the youngest of the Alpha Team, busily squeezing out another pimple on his callow face as he spoke. 'She didn't half have a pair of lungs on her! Biggest bristols–'

'*Shut up!*' chorused the rest of the Team. Rogers had been regaling them with lurid accounts of his sexual exploits in half the ports of the Western hemisphere ever since they had sailed from Portsmouth forty-eight hours before and they were sick of him.

'Can't think of nothing else but nookie, can yer, Rogers,' sneered Corporal Vic Ramsbottom, known behind his back as 'Sheepsarse', in his slow Yorkshire way. 'Yer get on my wick with it, rabbiting on all the time.'

'All right, Ramsbottom,' Mallory interrupted hastily, 'let's get on with the briefing, shall we? After all,' he looked around the faces of his Team, hollowed out to death's heads in the eerie, glowing light of the little submarine, 'we do have a rather pressing engagement soon.'

There was a murmur from the men of Alpha Team, then they fell silent.

'Well,' the Number One continued, 'this is

13

the situation. Our target is right on the far end of the harbour, sufficiently well away from the rest of the holiday craft to ensure that when the *accident* happens, no innocent party will get hurt.'

'Innocent!' Ross began with a sneer, but Mallory silenced him with one flash of those blue eyes.

'Can we see it?' Mallory asked.

'Of course,' the Number One agreed hastily. 'Here, in almost exactly the same spot where you-know-what happened.'

Mallory's face hardened. He nodded. 'I know,' he said softly, and at that moment the Number One could see the killer look on the younger man's face and felt a cold finger of fear trace its way down the small of his back. He refrained from shuddering only by a conscious effort.

'There she is,' continued the Number One, pointing to the left of the big glossy print. 'Registered in Boston, of course, and flying the Stars and Stripes.'

'And carrying enough high explosive to blow up the Falls Road for good,' Mallory said softly.

'Exactly. Now as far as we have been able to establish, she's crewed by five men and women. All of them have American passports, though MI6 is pretty sure that they're fake or bought on the black market. No matter – *officially*, they're American citizens. So–'

'So, we proceed with the utmost caution. We can't have all my fellow Old Etonians at the FO caught with their knickers round their ankles, can we?'

'Certainly not,' the naval officer agreed with a smile. 'The gentlemen of the FO are a fragile breed at the best of times.'

'Soft friggin' nellies!' snarled Ross, little red eyes glittering angrily. 'They can tattoo the Stars and Stripes on their jackseys, as far as I'm concerned. For my money they're a bunch of bluidy IRA murderers. We should waste 'em like they waste our lads in Northern Ireland!'

'Restrain yourself, Ross,' Mallory chided him mildly, knowing just how much Ross hated what he considered Mallory's 'toffee-nosed blether', and 'namby-pamby' atti-tudes. 'They will be duly *wasted*, as you wanted. But the important thing now is to consider *how* they are to be wasted!'

By way of response, the sergeant muttered something under his breath, and Rams-bottom's big, broad, honest Yorkshire face creased into a frown. 'What do you mean sir? They're gun-runners, sir, and we're supposed to take them out, like.'

'Banjo Irish fellows!' Bin Bahadur agreed eagerly, his dark, slanting eyes sparkling at the prospect of violent action.

Mallory took a last look at the photo, showing the Boston-registered craft silhouetted neatly against the background of the saw-toothed Donegal mountains. For a moment it was as if he were trying to imprint it on his mind for ever. Then he turned back to his team. 'Let me tell you a little tale first,' he said quietly. The men frowned, and again Ross grumbled under his breath obscenely. 'One August Bank Holiday five years ago now, a man who I personally admired a great deal, as did, I think, the Navy and our Corps of Marines – after all, he had been head of both services at one time–' Next to him, Number One, his face suddenly very serious, nodded his agreement. '–Came down from that castle up on the rocks, his family home, with a party of friends and relatives, took the path down to Mullaghmore Village, and boarded his motor-cruiser. *Shadow V*, it was called.'

As he listened, Ramsbottom's face began to light up slowly, as if the name meant something to him.

'It was a beautiful day,' Mallory continued. 'According to the press reports, there was a faint off-shore wind, a calm sea, and brilliant sunshine. In other words, ideal sailing weather for a man who was pushing eighty.' Suddenly Mallory bit his bottom lip and the Number One could see the cynical look had vanished from the young Marine officer's blue eyes; Mallory was obviously still very moved by what had happened out there in the Bay all those years ago. 'But the old admiral never did sail out of the Bay. As soon as he started up the engines, it happened! The IRA bully-boys had planted five pounds of gelignite in a long tube beneath the decking, between the cockpit and the engine. It went off like a 105-millimetre shell exploding. When the police recovered the body later, most of the left leg was gone, and his poor old frame was riddled and ripped apart by wood splinters. And he wasn't the only one. The kids and women went with him, too.' He stopped suddenly and stared hard around at the suddenly tense faces of his men. 'For a time, that old man had once commanded our own unit, back in the Old War. He was still colonel-commandant of the Royal Marines on the day he was so brutally murdered. If you don't know his name, I'll tell you.' Now there was iron in Mallory's voice and his eyes flashed fire. *'He was Admiral of Fleet, Earl Louis Mountbatten!'*

There was a gasp from the team, and even the ratings, tensed over their instruments in the control room of the submarine, risked a momentary glance at the tense, hunched marines of the Special Boat Service.

'That cruel assassination has been crying out for revenge these last five years,' Mallory went on. 'Of course, the weak sisters of the FO wouldn't buy it. But up top in the government, things have changed since 1979. We've got the green light, and we're going to waste those gun-runners in exactly the same way that they wasted Lord Louis – *and in exactly the same spot!'*

'When?' Ross asked eagerly, his eyes shining now, his thin lips drawn back in an almost wolfish grin, to reveal his long yellow teeth.

'Tomorrow morning – in full view of the holiday makers. That way, they can spread the word that the Brits still pay off old scores,' Mallory said grimly. 'And it'll happen at eleven-thirty precisely, the exact time that they gunned down Lord Louis.'

'But tomorrow, sir,' Corporal Ramsbottom gasped, finding his voice at last, 'is August—'

'Yes – August Bank Holiday!' Mallory beat the big bluff Yorkshireman to it. 'And for five IRA terrorists, it's not going to be a very happy one.'

'The women, too, sir?' Ramsbottom asked, looking worried.

'Dinna be a soft nelly!' Ross sneered. 'Them IRA bints are as hard as bluidy nails!'

'Yes, the women, too, Corporal,' Mallory barked, while the Number One looked down at his well-polished shoes, as if he did not want to know any more. Such things were better left to the professional killers.

'All right then, chaps,' Mallory continued, indicating with a quick flash of those bright cynical eyes of his that he did not need the Number One any more; that now they were beginning the 'wet business'. 'This is how C wants us to go about it...'

Up top it began to darken, and the little submarine started to rock as the waves mounted. Soon it would be night, and Alpha Team, the Special Boat Service, could go into action once more.

2

A brisk wind blew across the entrance to the bay, whipping up dull-white spurts of spray. Locked to the sinister black shape of the little diesel sub, the dinghy rocked back and forth as the two submariners attempted to steady it ready for the Alpha Team. Faintly from over at the holiday village came the strains of fiddle and accordion music. It was Saturday night in the Irish Republic and the usual *kali* dance was under way.

Mallory pulled on his black rubber face mask, shivering a little in the cold air after the heat of the sub's interior. Around him on the slightly rolling deck, his men prepared themselves for the mission, brisk and businesslike as usual, professionals to the man.

Mallory nodded his approval. They were a mixed bunch: Ross, with his tough, abrasive slum roughness; Rogers, the baby of the team, 'as randy as a bluidy goat,' as Ross always snarled, 'wi' a cock in the place o' a head'... But they were utterly trustworthy and dependable in a tight corner, each man a specialist in his own right.

'All right,' he said quietly, checking their equipment automatically in the faint light, as they finished buckling on their air tanks, 'I'll go over it quickly one more time. The matelots,' he indicated the two sailors trying to steady the rubber dinghy, 'will row us to the entrance to the harbour. We dive there and continue underwater all the way to the ship. Sergeant Ross and Rogers, you'll surface aft and fix the plastic to the screws. Ramsbottom and I will take the sharp end.'

No one smiled. Now their nerves had taken over and they were too wound up. All of them knew what was waiting for them if they were discovered. At the worst, the IRA thugs would kill them there and then and dump them over the side. At the best, the Irish court would slap a long sentence of hard labour on them in one of the Republic's gaols – and none of them had any illusions about how long they would survive once it became known that they were 'Brits'.

'What about Gunga Din here?' Ross asked, jerking a thumb at a shivering Rifleman Bin Bahadur.

Bahadur grinned, in no way offended by

Ross. Though skinny and seemingly frail, he possessed more stamina and staying power than the rest of them put together, and ironically was the only man in the team that Ross ever seemed to get along with.

'Bahadur goes on board and acts as look-out,' Mallory answered. 'According to our people on shore, on Saturday nights the crew goes on shore for the local entertainment.'

'Crikey,' Ramsbottom protested in his ponderous Yorkshire manner. 'Funny lot o' terrorists, they are. Leaving a shipload of high explosive unguarded while they go off for a knees-up!'

'They're Micks, aren't they?' Ross sneered. 'Thick as two planks. Ain't got sense enough to come in outa the rain!'

Mallory checked his air-intake nozzle. 'They feel safe enough from the land. They've got their people everywhere in Mullaghmore, keeping their eyes peeled for them. That's why we're coming in from the sea. They won't expect that.' He paused momentarily and stared around at their faces, white blurs set off by the tight black rubber hoods. 'One last thing, chaps. If we do bump into opposition, remember: there's to be no messing. There's got to be absolutely no evidence, at least for the general public, of how this thing was carried out.'

'Waste 'em!' Ross snapped.

'Exactly. All right, then. Let's go.'

Obediently they trooped after Mallory to the waiting boat, awkward in their flippers and heavy gear, to be helped into the dinghy one by one like stiff old men.

'Cast off!' whispered the Number One, his gaze fixed anxiously on the twinkling lights of the little holiday resort, whence the faint strains of *'Danny Boy'* wafted out on the breeze. 'And good luck.'

'Thank you, sir,' Mallory answered, as the two sailors pushed off and began to row. Moments later they had disappeared into the darkness and the Number One was clambering back onto the conning tower and counting his blessings; subs were a low-risk business in comparison with what the SBS types were about to tackle...

Mallory flashed a look to left and right, as the sea-wall protecting the little anchorage loomed ever larger out of the darkness, its sole illumination the marker buoy bobbing up and down gently in the waves. He nodded to the sweating matelots. 'Thanks, chaps, we're in close enough. Tuck yourself close to that buoy. With luck, we should be

back within the hour. If we're not...'
Mallory left the rest of his sentence unsaid.

The senior rating swallowed hard. 'Ay, ay, sir. We'll be here.'

Mallory readied his face mask, feeling his nerves tingling electrically with tension. Soon he and the rest of Alpha Team would be committed irrevocably. 'All right, chaps, here we go!' He slapped on his mask, poised himself on the edge of the dinghy for an instant and then flung himself backwards, to disappear into the Atlantic with a soft splash.

Swiftly the rest of the team followed, one by one. One moment they were there, the next they were gone. A splash. A burst of angry white water. A flurry of excited bubbles popping on the surface. Then nothing. Just the slow, heaving dark-green of the Atlantic.

The senior rating turned to his oppo in the darkness and said in a low, excited voice, as if he half-expected some IRA thug to peer over the edge of the streaming sea-wall at any moment, 'What a way to earn a living, eh, Jenkins? Banjoing a lot of Micks in the middle of the night. Sod that for a tale!' He shivered dramatically. 'All right, mate, put yer back into it. Let's get over to that friggin' buoy before we're spotted.'

'Stick a broom up my arse, Leading Hand, and I'll sweep the floor as I go out,' Jenkins grumbled, but suddenly he too was seized by the eerie tension of the summer night and began to row for the cover of the buoy with a will, breathing hard, as if the devil himself were behind him.

Meanwhile, Mallory swam easily, some twelve feet beneath the surface, hardly aware that he was swimming, his sole concern the green-glowing needle of his underwater compass strapped to his wrist, as he steered Alpha Team to their objective. The water was calm now, and he judged that they were inside the bay. It had become dirtier, too, with little bits of suspended matter floating by his mask, and once or twice the silver flash of eels scavenging for waste dropped overboard by holidaymakers messing about in boats this holiday week-end.

For a moment or two, Mallory wondered if there could be conger eels in this part of the world. The conger loved holes in harbour walls, and any frogman unfortunate enough to place his hand near one of them could get badly bitten. Once a conger had hooked its teeth into flesh or muscle, it would never let go. It used its body in jerks to tear off the flesh in which its jaws were embedded. They said that you could cut a conger's head off from its body, but its jaws would remain firmly sunk into the flesh of its victim and would have to be prized open after its death.

Hurriedly Mallory dismissed the subject from his mind and concentrated on controlling the flow of pearly bubbles escaping from his mask, which glowed in the darkness and might give away his position to a keen-eyed observer. He wanted no slips on this mission. As that grey-haired old spymaster had warned him, 'We want absolutely no publicity at all, Mallory! Her Majesty's Government could not be seen to be involved in the cold-blooded murder of American citizens, could they now? All we want is that the IRA knows we're after them and that we'll stop at nothing to pay them back for their crimes. In and out, Mallory, that's the motto. In and out, leaving behind only dead men – dead men who'll tell no tales!' And he had given that odd eerie, dry little chuckle of his that had sent an icy chill of fear down the young Marine's spine.

Mallory checked his compass bearing. Around him, his men came to a halt, treading water like strange rubbery fish. He nodded and with his free hand indicated that he was going up and that they should wait till he signalled.

Ross nodded his understanding, his face red and angry even behind the thick glass of the goggles.

Cautiously, very cautiously, Mallory began to ascend to the surface, breathing consciously now so as not to betray his position.

Suddenly he started. Something was coming towards him! His free hand flashed to the knife strapped to his right leg. Next instant he relaxed. It was an old jacket that someone had tossed over the side of one of the holiday boats. It wafted by him, followed by a trail of plastic beer cans, the empty arms moving grotesquely, as if waving to him. Then it was gone, and Mallory was trying to calm his frantically racing heart, scolding himself for behaving like some rookie straight out of diving school.

A moment later he broke the surface of the harbour with a slight plop. The IRA boat, the Stars and Stripes hanging limply at her stern, was directly in front of him, perhaps fifty yards away. He was dead on course!

For a few seconds he trod water as he

surveyed the scene. The front was ablaze with lights and he could hear the tinny Irish dance music quite clearly. Cars moved slowly across the high road above the harbour and he could see the long white beams of their headlights as they turned inland. All was normal; a typical August Saturday evening. The good people of Mullaghmore would all be in the pubs or clustered around their TVs, watching whatever Radio Reflis had to offer this particular evening.

Mallory nodded to himself, as if in approval, took one last glance at the target vessel, which was blacked out from stem to stern, and dived again to inform the others.

Now the four of them set to work, while Rifleman Bahadur hauled himself up onto the deck noiselessly and crouched in the cluttered bow, black unwinking eyes fixed on the shore as if his life depended upon it.

Below, Mallory worked on the screws, packing the plastic in little lumps along the shaft and inserting the time-pencils. He hoped they would be more accurate than most, for he dearly wanted the IRA ship to disintegrate five years to the very minute after the treacherous murder of Earl Mountbatten. All the same, he wasn't taking any chances. In case the IRA thugs did decide to set sail before then, the charges packed around the screws would go off immediately. It was no use the ship being blown up at sea. The explosion *had* to be seen from the land, so that the word would get out: that at long last the Brits had taken their revenge for Lord Louis! Steadily he and the others worked at their task, aware of the familiar pain at the back of the neck, as if icy cold water was trickling in through a hole in the suit and wetting their neck and shoulders; and as always, each man of the Alpha Team swore that *next time* he'd remember to put on an extra woollen sweater.

Up above, Rifleman Bahadur was not worried by such considerations. His skinny body, hardened by the poverty and the rigours of his barren, mountainous Nepalese homeland, seemed to feel neither cold nor heat. Fatigue was a stranger to Bahadur as well. He could have crouched there all night without making the slightest movement, searching that shore with his keen eyes, until finally Mallory relieved him. But it was not to be.

The sound was vague and low, but his acute hearing caught it. His every muscle tensed, his heart beating like a trip-hammer as he located its source. He turned – and in

29

the very same instant a brawny naked arm crooked itself around his skinny neck and his nostrils were assailed by the stink of cheap scent and woman.

Instinctively, he jabbed back his elbow. It slammed into the soft flesh of a breast. There was a sharp intake of breath and he jabbed again, just as the air began to go from his lungs and the first red stars started to explode in front of his eyes.

'*Bastard*!' the woman gasped, and the pressure slackened.

Bahadur ducked swiftly, still on his knees, and turning round, tried to get up.

An enormous woman loomed up in front of him in the glowing darkness. Her hair was loose and hanging around her shoulders, her monstrous body clad in a tent-like, dirty white nylon nightdress, through which her massive dugs hung like deflated balloons. She was barefoot.

The apparition stopped even the little Gurkha. '*Woman*?!' he gasped stupidly, and let his mouth fall open like a stranded fish. His hands dropped to his sides.

The huge woman thrust out a hand like a small steam shovel and as he knelt there, gawping like a village yokel, her fingers settled on his testicles and stabbed sadistically into the soft secret flesh. Her face contorted with rage and pleasure, the sweat streaming down the white pudding-cheeks, she hissed, 'Now I've got yer, boyo, to be sure!' Exerting all her strength, she twisted cruelly.

Bahadur nearly passed out. His lower body was aflame with agony. Hot bitter bile flooded his throat and he only managed to prevent himself screaming by biting his bottom lip till the blood came. In a minute she'd rip them off.

The woman grunted and heaved. Bahadur found himself being flung off his feet. He had to do something – and fast. Once that enormous bulk descended upon his skinny frame, he'd be finished.

Now, as the blood-red mist threatened to swamp him and his ears were filled with the mad rushing of unconsciousness, he sought her face with his free hand. Time and time again, she dodged his searching fingers, mumbling terrible obscenities through gritted teeth as she exerted that horrible, killing pressure on his sexual organs. In a minute he'd black out. *He had to find her nose*!

Suddenly he had it. She dodged too late, her face glistening as if it had been greased with vaseline, her breath coming in harsh, hectic sobs. Her eyes bulged out of her pudding face like those of a mad woman. Bahadur straightened his two forefingers to steel prongs like he had been taught and hesitated no longer. Time was running out. He thrust them home.

The woman's scream was stifled by an explosion of pain as Bahadur rammed his fingers deep inside her nose. Next moment he ripped up and outwards, feeling his hand flush with hot wet blood. His temples throbbing madly, the blood-red mist swamping him, he held on with the very last of his strength. *Would the monster never let go of his penis?*

Suddenly the little man, his face contorted by sheer agony, felt his fingers beginning to slip. Desperately he held on. The woman was screaming now ... screaming ... screaming. He must silence her. *He must!* With the last of his strength, feeling his head reel, he chopped down his free hand on her shoulder.

It did the trick. Suddenly that terrible grip was released. Bahadur staggered back against the bulkhead, holding his crotch with fingers that were wet and sticky with blood, gasping for breath as if he had just run a great race, while his antagonist reeled to a winch, blood streaming down her fat chin to drip unheeded on her nightgown, her massive dugs heaving mightily as if they might burst through the flimsy material of their own volition.

For what seemed an age, the two of them slumped there, eyeing each other malevolently like two old pugs who had battled each other through fourteen terrible rounds and were now preparing desperately for the fifteenth.

'Hoor's son!' she gasped thickly, her mouth full of blood, 'I'm gonna … kill you!' Frantically her fat fingers sought a weapon, while Bahadur, his lower body aflame with burning pain, seemed unable to move, still trapped by that terrible, overwhelming hurt.

On the shore someone was singing drunkenly in a cockney accent, *'Have yer never bin across the sea to Ireland… Have yer never seen the…'*

'I'm gonna cut you … *for good*!' the woman hissed, levering up her massive bulk.

Something glinted in the faint silver light and Bahadur's heart skipped a beat. In her ham of a fist was clasped what looked like a meat cleaver. *Still* he could not move. That terrible pain seemed to have paralysed his lower limbs.

Slowly, the cleaver raised, she staggered towards him, the front of her nightdress wet and red with blood, mouthing obscenities to herself as she came in for the kill, eyes wide and staring with crazed bloodlust.

'*Banjo*' a little voice at the back of Bahadur's mind commanded urgently, '*Banjo!*'

As if in a dream, his fingers sought the weapon strapped to his leg. The woman was almost on to him now. He could smell her stink and the cheap scent with which she attempted to hide it. Her massive bulk seemed to fill the whole night. 'Hoor's son!' she chanted, as if it were some kind of sacred ritual, 'Hoor's son...'

From the land, the drunken Cockney wailed on. '...*Going across the sea to dear old Ireland...*'

'*Now die!*' she screamed suddenly, voice high, hysterical, and triumphant, eyes glittering with madness, as she raised the cleaver high above her head with both hands, her breasts shooting upwards under the silky material.

With the last of his strength, the little man lunged forward. The knife plunged deep into that soft stomach, and for one long moment the little man and the enormous woman were fused thus, frozen in a melodramatic tableau of love and death. Then suddenly Bahadur, sobbing for breath now, withdrew the knife with a terrible sucking noise. For one instant more the woman towered above him, the madness gone from her eyes now, face suddenly softened and at ease, like that of a woman satisfied by the act of love. The cleaver tumbled from her suddenly nerveless fingers and clattered to the deck. Slowly, very slowly, like a carefully deflated balloon, she began to sink to the deck.

Across on the quay, the drunken Cockney launched into *The Rose of Donegal*...

3

'*Caps off*!' the CPO barked.

Quite smartly for submariners, the ratings on the deck of the little diesel sub whipped off their white caps and thrust them beneath their arms. The men of Alpha Team stiffened to attention in best Royal Marine fashion. Out of the side of his mouth, Sergeant Ross whispered to a still shaken and rather green-looking Rifleman Bahadur, 'It's all right, Gunga Din.'

The captain, bareheaded, braid cap under his arm, Bible in his gloved hands, advanced on the waiting crew slowly, while overhead the sun shone benignly down on the slow rollers of the Atlantic.

Pausing, he announced in a tight, clipped voice, 'I shall not read the burial service over her. For the same reason that I ordered she should *not* be covered with the Union flag.' He indicated the corpse wrapped solely in a body bag, the weights already attached to the naked yellow feet. 'We are at war with her kind. They are the enemy – an enemy who do not believe in God, in spite of all their protests to the contrary. Their God lies in Moscow.' He let his words sink in, staring around at their young pale faces, his own set, hard and old.

Mallory, standing in front of his men, could well imagine the captain as one of those stern 19th-century missionaries who went out to convert the heathen, armed with a Bible in one hand and a rifle in the other. He could well believe the story that the captain had patrolled off the Argentine coast for a hundred and fifty days during the Falklands War, just waiting for a crack at the Argies' aircraft-carrier. He had still been there when the Argies had surrendered.

'Instead, I shall simply commend her soul to God,' he continued, 'and her body to the deep. Chief Petty Officer!'

'Sir!'

'Cast the body over the side!'

Behind Mallory, the little Gurkha tensed, the memory of that terrible fight in the darkness still all too fresh in his mind. How he had managed to force himself to clean up the blood and slip over the side to where the others waited to tow her out to the waiting dinghy, he would never know.

Two brawny submariners eased the bag

with the body over the side of the sub. A splash and it was gone, down to the depths of the Atlantic.

The captain stared at the spot for a moment reflectively, his lean face dark and sombre, then he replaced his cap, the CPO commanded, 'Caps *on*!' and the brief funeral was over.

The captain looked at his watch and turned to stare at the faint smudge on the horizon which was Ireland. 'A minute to go,' he announced.

Mallory and the rest of the team tensed. In sixty seconds they would know whether their plan had succeeded or failed. But suppose the disappearance of the fat woman had made the others suspect?

'Thirty seconds!' the captain snapped.

'*Fifteen*!'

'Five ... *zero*!'

Exactly on time, there was a faint pink flash on the horizon, followed an instant later by a thick, black mushroom of oily smoke ascending to the bright August sun. From the direction of the land there came a muted boom like a big drum being struck a long way off.

'*Hurrah*!' A ragged cheer broke out spontaneously, and suddenly the SBS men were slapping each other on the back, with even Sergeant Ross attempting a craggy, wintry smile and young Rogers urging, 'Go on, Sarge, give yer ears a treat – *smile*!'

The captain's hard, lean face relaxed as he held up his hand for silence. 'Well, lads, it's done,' he said. 'Not a nice thing, I'll admit, but it isn't a perfect world. At least we've shown them that the Royal Navy – with a little assistance from the Royal Marines–' he smiled at Mallory – 'can pay back a debt to one of its own kind. If it's got to be fight fire with fire, we'll show the bastards what the old Royal can do! All right, CPO, dismiss the ship's company.' The captain turned to Mallory. 'Lieutenant, could I speak to you a moment?'

The captain waited till the deck had cleared and the ratings had headed back to their duties before he spoke. 'Mallory, I've just had an urgent signal before I came up topside, concerning you and your chaps.'

'Sir?'

The captain frowned. 'We're to go back to Pompey. But without you, it appears.'

Now it was Mallory's turn to frown. 'I don't quite understand, sir.'

'Neither do I really, Mallory. But my orders are to proceed under water from now onwards and land you and your chaps before dawn on Tuesday morning on the Yorkshire coast.'

'*Yorkshire coast*!' Mallory exclaimed. 'But what are we going to do in the wilds of Yorkshire? I mean, sir, what kind of mission could the powers that be possibly find for us up there?'

The captain favoured the younger man with a wintry smile. 'It's not a mission – *yet*,' he explained. 'I'm to land you at a designated spot between Withernsea, which is the last township on the Yorkshire coast before the Humber Estuary, and the village of Easington. There, you'll be met.'

'Met? Met by whom, sir?' Mallory asked, not a little irritated. He had intended applying for a short leave after this IRA thing was finished. He had recently met a little American number in the Big Smoke who had been very liberal with her favours – and she had plenty to be liberal with! He had hoped he could have sampled more of the same.

The captain hesitated a fraction of a second. 'You're going to receive a very high honour, young Mallory, for a chap of your rank,' he said.

'Sir?'

'You are indeed!' Instinctively, the captain looked round the deck as if to ensure that they were not being observed. 'You're going to be received by no less a person than ... *C himself*!' he whispered.

Mallory's mouth dropped open stupidly. It wasn't every day that humble lieutenants, even if they were engaged in covert operations, were met by the Head of British Intelligence. *'Christ!'* he gasped. *'Then the shit really must have hit the fan*! Er – excuse my French, sir,' he added hastily.

But the captain seemed not to notice. He nodded his head sagely, his faded light blue eyes gazing out on the dancing waves, as if he could see something there visible only to himself. 'That it does, Mallory, that it does, indeed...'

'That's put the sodding boot in it, hasn't it!' Rogers complained, as he slipped into a startling scarlet sweater, decorated with the blazing white legend, *Frogmen Do It Underwater*. 'I had this date with a chick in Pompey for next Wednesday. Holiday Inn and dinner by candlelight, the works. She was paying, of, course,' he added, as if it were the most obvious thing in the world. 'Then open up them pearly gates! Now, it's all sodding off!' He shook his head sadly. 'I don't know, this is ruining my sex life.' He pulled the sweater straight and admired himself in the little steel shaving mirror attached to the submarine's bulkhead. 'Not bad, eh? I like to be a bit of a trendsetter with my threads.'

Corporal Ramsbottom looked up from his *Playboy* centrefold and said straight-faced, 'You look more like a bleeding *Irish* setter to me!'

Lying on his bunk, a map of France in his hands, Mallory grinned lazily. The men were in good heart, in spite of the uncertainty of this new assignment to darkest Yorkshire. When he had told them the news, they had accepted it without complaint, save for Corporal Ramsbottom, who had commented, 'Hope they're not expecting us to scuttle the People's Republic of South Yorkshire, sir. My old Dad still lives in Sheffield. He'd do his nut if he ever heard I voted conservative!' Only Ross had asked the obvious question, and Mallory had been forced to tell him that he knew nothing except that they were going to meet someone very important from London Intelligence and that it might have something to do with France.

'France?' Ross had queried. 'I don't like the Frogs. They eat friggin' snails!'

'They eat other things as well, Ross,' Rogers had said quickly, rolling his eyes and simpering in what he fondly imagined to be a French accent, 'Oh, la, la!'

Ross had ignored the pimply-faced Marine and had stared challengingly at Mallory, as if demanding an answer.

Mallory had shrugged a little helplessly. 'You know as much as me, Ross,' he had explained. 'All I know is that the signal the captain received also directed me to study the map of France – and the French canal system in particular.'

Lying in his bunk and listening to the steady throb of the *Daring*'s motors as the sub bore them ever closer to their rendez-vous and the banter of his men as they changed into their civvies, ready for the landing, Mallory frowned and wondered, too; *why France?*

What did it all mean? he asked himself, staring moodily at the blue rash of lines that covered the country from north to south, representing France's extensive river-canal system. Here they were, right up to the necks in the IRA thing – they had been carrying out covert ops against the Irish terrorists for six months now – and now suddenly they were summoned in this mysterious fashion to Yorkshire, away from the IRA scene altogether, possibly for an assignment which had something to do with France. Why else the order to study the French waterways. *What the hell was going on?*

4

The whistle shrilled. Almost immediately, the hooded, lean figure burst out of the house, running full pelt, Heckler and Koch MP5 clutched tightly to his hip, sweating under the weight of a huge Bergin rucksack and looking like a multicoloured hunchback in his camouflaged gear.

'Shoot'n scoot training,' cried the immensely tall SAS brigadier above the thunder and flash of the simulator grenades exploding on both sides of the running man. 'Hit 'em hard, fast and lethally, and then do a bunk double-quick!'

The little grey-faced civilian, dwarfed by Mallory and the SAS brigadier, clapped his hands together with delight. 'How exciting!' he exclaimed.

The SAS trooper skidded to a halt next to the locked door of the training house. Behind him, another hooded figure raised the heavy Remington shotgun. At fifty yards off, he pulled the trigger. There was a tremendous boom. The first man didn't even flinch as a great charge of live ammunition hissed by him and slammed into the wooden door. The air was full of splinters as the door flew open, to sag drunkenly on its hinges.

The hooded man didn't wait for a second invitation. A 'flash-bang' flew from his free hand to explode with an ear-splitting crump and a flash of purple light, and then he was in, his little German-made machine pistol with its curved magazine chattering away hysterically as he slaughtered the imaginary terrorists inside. A second later he was out again and belting from cover, leaving behind him a grey wisp of smoke from the shattered room.

The brigadier slapped the knob of his stop-watch. 'Not bad! Thirty seconds. Not bad at all... But of course, they'll have to do better than that when they're fully trained.' He looked down his big nose at Mallory. 'In the SAS we can't be amateurish about these things like you chaps from the gyreens,* you know, Mallory. Two years training before we even start considering them for an operation. Not like you tip-toe boys from Poole.** A couple of weeks of mucking about in boats

*Pun on the word 'marines'
**Headquarters of the Special Boat Service

and a bit of swimming in the local corporation baths and you're off on ops, what?'

'Come, come, John,' the little grey civilian chided the brigadier. 'You mustn't pull rank on Mallory like that.' He winked at Mallory, who was still wondering why he had been brought to this former airfield in wildest Yorkshire and recovering from a crazy predawn ride through deserted country lanes. 'I'm sure that you chaps of the SBS do at least *four* weeks of training, what?' He grinned, and the brigadier grinned back. 'Well, I'll leave you, sir. The place is one hundred percent secure. The Special Branch people are patrolling the outer perimeter,' he indicated the rusting wire fence in the distance beyond the grass-overgrown RAF huts and the windswept desolate runways, 'and my own chaps are securing the inner perimeter. You'll be safe enough here – unless of course the opposition has got something like Mallory's outfit which can come up through the drains, what?' He winked at Mallory, and then, as the chatter and clatter of helicopters coming in from the North Sea indicated that the second part of the SAS training exercise was about to start, he saluted hurriedly and doubled to the cracked runway, followed by his bandy-legged bodyguard, armed with his shotgun.

To the rear, Sergeant Ross sneered, 'Bluidy lot of poofters! I swear that one of yon heroes was using a deodorant!'

'Ay, but they do serve a nice bit o' grub,' chimed in Ramsbottom, wiping the grease from his unshaven chin and belching appreciatively. 'That cook of theirs gave me two fried eggs without even being asked. Now yer can't beat that, Sarge, even if they are a lot of nancyboys.'

Mallory shook his head. He was glad that the big Yorkshireman wasn't making his comments in the saloon bar, otherwise there would have been a right old punch-up. The SAS troopers were very touchy about their reputation for toughness.

The little grey civilian took Mallory by the arm and began to steer him away from the team towards one of the abandoned RAF buildings. 'I'm sure that you and your chaps are wondering what all this is about, Mallory, eh? The strange landing, the drive through the night to this somewhat chilly spot...' He shivered. 'I often wonder what God was doing when he created Yorkshire. I swear it can't be any colder in the Arctic at this moment.'

'It is a bit parky, sir,' Mallory said, as the choppers came clattering in for the practice assault, the SAS trainees already swarming down the ladders, although they were still three hundred feet or more off the ground.

'Of course, Mallory,' the little civilian raised his voice above the racket, 'you've been there. And then all this blood and thunder.'

He led Mallory inside the old RAF building, which still stank of oil, human sweat and old wars. On the wall, there was a fading, crude drawing of a man with no trousers and below him the words, *It's no use standing on the seat. The crabs in this place jump six feet*!'

The civilian caught the direction of Mallory's gaze and laughed softly. 'Pop art, I'd suppose they call it these days. We used to do that sort of thing all the time in the Old War.'

Mallory looked down at the little man with his grey hair, grey face and grey clawlike hands. It was almost as if he was already half-dead and crumbling to dust. Could he ever have drawn graffiti like that or have even been involved in something so animal and alive as a war? Somehow he couldn't quite imagine it.

The man known as C led him inside and indicated that Mallory should take a seat on one of the two camp chairs which had been set up in the empty, debris-littered room, its ceiling still covered with the fading, yellowed pictures of 1940s starlets. 'Crotch art, *we* used to call it,' C said, with a grey smile, which seemed to make his jaw muscles creak with the effort. He sat down heavily and huddled the overcoat around him in that cold, cheerless place, the thin rays of the August sun slanting in through the broken windows.

'A cover operation, Mallory,' he said after a moment, thin face frowning. 'Yesterday I flew to Bradbury Lines* and then came out with the brigadier and his chaps. I thought whoever is watching my office would assume that it was legitimate for the head of MI6 to visit the SAS and then proceed to view one of their training exercises. After all, our two services do, as you know, work very closely together on certain missions.' He smiled a soft, secret smile, as if he had just thought of something which gave him a certain cold pleasure. 'Sad, though, when one comes to think of it, that I have to go to

*SAS Headquarters at Hereford

such lengths to meet you, what?'

Mallory nodded, not really understanding what was going on. 'But, sir, if I may ask – why all the subterfuge?'

C shrugged. 'The usual thing these days in London, I suppose – unfortunately. A leak. Probably several damned leaks!'

Outside, the SAS men hit the tarmac, hard. Already they were pelting down the runway, snapping off shots to left and right, white tracer zipping above their heads, other live slugs ripping up little eruptions of concrete dust in front of their racing feet as they charged to the attack. Somewhere a hoarse, contemptuous voice was yelling above the clatter of the rotors and snap-and-crackle of the fire-fight, 'Come on now, move it! Spread them bleedin' legs! Nothing'll fall out – and if it does, I'll pick it up personally and hand-carry it to yer wimmin back in Hereford!' The voice laughed coarsely.

C sighed again. ''Twas ever thus,' he said vaguely.

Mallory grinned. He couldn't imagine this dried-up grey old man ever doing anything so violent as the assault course.

Suddenly the Head of Intelligence was very brisk and businesslike. 'Right, Mallory.

Down to cases. Why do I want you and your chaps?' He answered his own question. 'Bluebeard, that's why.'

'*Bluebeard*?' Mallory echoed, a little startled.

'Yes. Codename, of course. Russian. Leading man in the KGB. Dirty tricks department. Foreign Intelligence. Misinformation. Been everywhere. Knows everybody, right up to the very top.' Now C's phrases were coming out in a clipped kind of official shorthand. 'Real name, Serov, Yuri. Aged about fifty, fat, and foolish. The great lover, you see – with KGB money, naturally.'

'Naturally,' Mallory repeated mechanically.

'Always runs a strong team of mistresses. Black, brown, white, the colour of the season. The usual sort of thing for that kind of chap. Very low life.'

'Is that why they call him Bluebeard, sir?' Mallory prompted hopefully, completely mystified now.

Outside, one of the hooded SAS troopers was going straight up a sheer wall without a rope, scuttling up it effortlessly like a monkey, while the hoarse voice of the instructor bellowed, *'Come on Number Five!*

Get a soding move on!… I've got a date with a very hot body in two hours' time… Move!'

'Not exactly.' Again C favoured the younger man with that wintry, rusty smile. 'You see, he's such a high man in their organisation that the KGB can't allow his ladyfriends to run around loose afterwards.'

'You mean they imprison them, sir?'

'No.' C looked coy. *'They liquidate them!'*

Mallory's mouth dropped open stupidly and C grinned, obviously pleased with the effect of his words.

'Good grief, sir, you mean – like the *real* Bluebeard?'

'I do, Mallory. That French chappie who did for all his wives at the turn of the century. The man's a monster. So is his organisation. Pillow talk, the KGB thinks, might endanger the glorious future of the Workers' and Peasants' Paradise. So, once Serov has finished with them, off they go. Quietly and discreetly. Accident with a fast car. Careless overdose of sleeping pills. Drowning at some southern resort. The usual KGB wet business. Nasty, but necessary. Always the same, though – and it boils down to *this*.' So saying, he crooked one of his clawlike fingers, the knuckles creaking audibly, as if he were pulling a trigger. 'And another little nubile popsy goes for a Burton!'

Mallory frowned.

C chuckled. 'How dreadfully antiquated I must sound to you, Mallory!' he exclaimed. 'All that Old War slang. *Popsy* and *going for a Burton*. I'm sure you must think I'm absolutely in my dotage? Should be put out to pasture and all that, what?'

Mallory thought nothing of the sort. The grey old man facing him, he knew, was as trendily ruthless and cold-blooded as the youngest CIA whizzkid from Georgetown or one of those remote training camps in Central America. 'But if I may try again, sir,' he said, while C dabbed his thin grey lips with a silk handkerchief, 'what have we to do with this Bluebeard chap?'

C tucked his handkerchief up his skinny sleeve and looked at Mallory in mock surprise. 'Tut, tut,' he chided, 'I thought a bright young chap like yourself would have already twigged it. Dearie me, there I go again with my out of date slang! Why, Lieutenant Mallory, you're going to do me a great favour. You're going to bring our Slavic Casanova back to England for me.' He beamed at the young Marine officer winningly. 'Now, what do you say to that?'

54

Outside, a percussion grenade exploded with an earsplitting boom and a shower of broken glass tinkled musically to the ground. But at that particular moment there was nothing very musical about it to Mallory's ears. Instead, it sounded vaguely like a knell of doom.

5

Hastily the Peeper squirmed deeper into the hot bracken and lay completely still, hardly noticing the nettles. Slowly the battered old van bearing the fading legend, *Jo's Video Shack, Thirsk*, crawled round the bend on the outside perimeter road. In the front could be seen two big, young, bearded men in donkey jackets, seemingly chatting aimlessly as they drove. In his hiding place the Peeper smiled to himself. Both of them were SB* men. The one was Chambers, the other, Horrocks, both detective sergeants.

He knew all about them, naturally. It was his profession. Chambers was a swinger, divorced, up to his eyes in debt, keeping one of those young black ravers that so many of the fuzz were acquiring these days, somewhere up in Holloway. Horrocks was different: semi-detached on a mortgage, up in the 'nicer' part of Camberwell, knocking his guts out with overtime so that he could

*Special Branch

56

send his only kid through St Paul's as a day-boy. Both were bastards of the first order who'd knee you in the balls as soon as look at you.

The van passed, and raising himself cautiously, the Peeper gave them the fingers contemptuously. The SB would have to get up earlier in the day if they wanted to catch him with his imitation black silk mini-briefs down, the Brit pigs!

Swiftly, the Peeper started to assemble the big telelens camera with practised ease, while a mile away on the derelict airfield the bullyboys of the SAS went through their lethal drills.

It had been the SB boys who had led him straight to this arsehole of a place. As soon as he had gotten the wire that C was leaving Century House, he had tacked on to his SB bodyguard at once. He had followed them right up the M1, off to the A1, and then down the winding little 'B' roads until they had reached this place; and as always, the fuzz hadn't suspected a thing. He wiped a bead of snot off his nose and slung it contemptuously into the bracken. Christ, it had been as easy as falling off a log! What a lot of shitehawks they all were! He patted the expensive Japanese camera and whispered, 'Now, camera-san, get Daddy some nice clear pix, eh? He needs lolly for the lovely boys this weekend.'

Rapidly, expertly, he began snapping the running hooded SAS men, trying to get a close-up – difficult as it was at that distance – of each man. They were hooded, of course, but the wogs of the PLO would pay even for poor photos of SAS men. After all, they had money to burn, and they had to show the Saudis they were doing something for all the oil-dough they were getting.

Next, the swarthy little man in the shabby clothes turned his attention to the two men barely visible through the shattered windows of what might once have been the Mess.

C he recognised immediately. 'Bejasus,' he told himself, 'I'd know the old tit-turd with my eyes closed!' After all, C and his movements formed his main source of income as a freelance observer. All of them were prepared to pay for *that* kind of info. But the other man was completely unknown to him. He certainly wasn't the fuzz. Neither was he SA-shitting-S. They all had the same kind of mugs, tough, cocky and obvious.

Delicately he adjusted the telephoto lens

and tried to get a clearer image, tongue stuck out of the corner of his mouth because it was tricky, wondering just what was going on over there on the field. 'Come on, C,' he said to himself in his soft Dublin burr, 'give us a clue for fuck's sake … I need the fucking money…'

'You see, Mallory,' C was saying, 'Bluebeard has finally met his match. In the very desirable form of Miss Jo-Jo Johns. An American lady, naturally, with that name. Formerly, she was what I believe is called a "go-go girl".' He put his skinny grey hand to his mouth politely, as if to muffle a belch. 'Now she's working for the CIA.' He reached inside his overcoat and passed Mallory a photograph.

The girl had one of those 'Californian' faces, bronzed, blonde, bold; all shining, even teeth, set in a perfect smile, with 'laughing' eyes. The figure was awe-inspiring and the tight-fitting silk sheath the girl was wearing concealed not a single one of those tremendously exciting curves and hollows. Obviously she was wearing no underwear. 'My God, sir,' Mallory stuttered, 'she's certainly got everything!' He licked suddenly dry lips.

'That she has, my boy,' C agreed. 'Didn't have girls like that when I was young, I'm afraid. Of course, it's all man-made, naturally.'

'*Man-made*?' Mallory echoed stupidly, not taking his eyes off Miss Johns' dizzying curves.

'Yes, she's a typical product of what they call the Californian Three-B Merchants – belly, bum and bosom. All the work of the plastic surgeon.' Abruptly C looked oddly embarrassed. 'They even rumour,' he whispered, dropping his gaze momentarily, 'that she has had something done to her – er – *thing* to make it look more interesting. Can't imagine what. But the mind boggles, doesn't it?'

'Boggle it does, sir,' Mallory agreed, reluctantly passing the photo back into C's outstretched claw.

'Well, Bluebeard has fallen head-over-heels for darling Jo-Jo Johns. Now he loves her with all the passionate ardour of his Slavic soul, unaware that she's a CIA plant. Oldest game in the world, and cynical and worldly-wise as we chaps in Intelligence are supposed to be, we fall for it all the time. Bluebeard, too. For her – and a life pension, naturally – he's prepared to give up everything – even the delights of the Soviet Paradise. She's the bait, and he's swallowed it hook, line and sinker.'

'Yes, sir,' Mallory said a little helplessly, 'but how does Alpha Team fit into an op being run by the CIA? They've got their own Green Berets, surely?'

Outside, an SAS trooper who had obviously fallen foul of his instructor, was hopping frantically up and down the tarmac, face crimson with effort, his Remington shotgun held out at arm's length, watched by an unsympathetic Alpha Team.

'Bluebeard is about to defect, Mallory,' C said. 'We have our sources in the CIA, too.' He smiled softly. 'There are moles burrowing away in Langley, too. Now, normally we would have no objection to an attempt by the CIA to nobble a Russian agent, save for one thing. Bluebeard knows about the moles in our own service. He already told the CIA about them when he put forward his sales list to them. After all, he wants a pension, as well as Jo-Jo.' Suddenly C's old grey face hardened. 'In the last few years, Mallory, the Service has taken some very hard knocks. Since that damned stuttering rogue Philby there's been one rotten scandal after another. Imagine what the reaction in Washington would be if Bluebeard starts spilling the beans about new failings in British security. The anti-British lobby, fed by organisations like Noraid* and similar groupings, is strong enough as it is. There would be several influential people over there who would be only too happy to insist that existing links between ourselves, the CIA and the NSA** should be severed immediately. That, I don't need to tell you, young man, would be a very serious situation indeed and one that no British government, even if it were run by the Trots, could tolerate. We always need to know what the US government is really up to, and we can only do that through co-operation with its secret services.'

He paused for breath, while outside the men of Alpha began a slow handclap, as the SAS trooper with the Remington started to slow down dramatically, the shotgun drooping ever lower in his outstretched hands. In a minute he would give up altogether and fall flat on his face. Desperately he tried to fight off the inevitable, knowing that it would mean disgrace. For

*Pro-IRA American organisation
**US National Security Agency

him it would be 'RTU'*, and the end of his career in the Special Air Service.

The little group of clapping, jeering civilians attracted the Peeper's interest. He swung the big Jap camera round and focused on the little scene being acted out on the runway. One by one, he snapped the faces of the jeering men. They seemed different from the SAS types. One was brown, for example, and one was far too young for the Special Air. He stopped suddenly as the legend on the youngster's bright-red sweater became visible in the glittering circle of glass. *'Frogmen do it underwater,'* he read out under his breath. Of course, it was another of those silly sweat-shirt slogans that young people liked to hang on their skinny chests to give themselves some sense of identity. But what was a frogman doing here? And why were he and the rest of them making fun of the SAS thug? Did they belong to some other Brit military outfit?

'Christ!' he cursed to himself. 'What's going on? Here C goes chasing off to this arsehole of the world and turns up with a frogman in a stupid non-regulation T-shirt,

* Returned to unit

63

a kid still wet behind the lugs. Yet the SAS put on a real big show to give him cover, including a fullblown brigadier.' He shrugged angrily. 'Christ, what a way to have to make a living!'

For a moment he lowered the heavy camera and indulged in his favourite daydream, in which he was lying on a sun-drenched Californian beach with a blond Adonis in tight slacks and black leather, complete with bronzed, bulging muscles and a handsome scowl that threatened all sorts of humiliating naughtiness...

A mile away, a worried Mallory, who a long time ago had ceased indulging in daydreams, was asking hurriedly, 'But are we expected to go into Russia and pick up Bluebeard before the Yanks get to him?'

'Of course not, my dear boy. Far too dangerous. Probably every village militiaman throughout the Workers' Paradise has got a copy of your photograph. You're all far too well known for that, believe you me. No. We let the CIA do the hard and dirty work of getting Bluebeard out of Russia for us. Then we must snatch him from under their very noses. Between the time he leaves Russia and before he starts the last leg of his journey to the United States, you grab him.'

He cleared his throat with a strange gurgling sound like that of an asthmatic in the throes of an attack. 'Naturally, Mallory, there must be no rough stuff. Nominally the CIA *is* our ally – in a way.' He gave Mallory his slow smile.

Mallory understood. It was the old oblique style that Intelligence always used; they could never say anything important straight out. That would never do. 'Yes, of course, sir,' he said. 'I understand.'

'Good. I'm glad. Wouldn't like to think that any of our cousins across the sea would come to any harm through excessive zeal on your part, what? Now then, your orders!'

'Sir?' Mallory tensed.

Outside the choppers were clattering down once more to end the exercise and pick up the troopers for the journey back to Hereford. Over on the field, the whistles shrilled urgently. Hoarse voices yelled orders. Exhausted ones responded. All was controlled confusion as the crimson-faced troopers in their balaclava hoods came running towards the choppers, chests heaving with effort, rucksacks bobbing up and down on their backs.

C rose and tugged a large buff-coloured envelope from inside his overcoat with a grey skeletal claw. 'Here,' he said, 'read them on the road to the port, Mallory. Then give them plenty of careful study on the boat.'

'What boat, sir?' Mallory asked, a little surprised, tucking the envelope away carefully.

'Why, my boy, after Q* has kitted you and your good fellows out, you're going on a cruise. A long, leisurely cruise, such as I suspect friend Bluebeard and his delightful paramour will be enjoying, courtesy of the CIA, in due course.' He smiled winningly at the younger man, though his faded grey eyes remained lifeless and cold. 'And they say one meets all sorts of exciting people and experiences and all sorts of exciting adventures on a long, leisurely cruise, don't they?' He pressed Mallory's hand with one that felt as cold as the grave. 'I must go now. The car is already waiting for you and your chaps. Goodbye and good luck, Mallory.'

'Thank you, sir,' Mallory said a little helplessly, stumbling to attention as the enormous figure of the SAS brigadier appeared at the door, as always accompanied by his bodyguard. 'When–' he ventured.

*Quartermaster section

But C was already gone, half-carried to the waiting chopper by the brigadier, his clothes flapping against his skinny limbs.

Now the choppers were beginning to ascend, hovering there like sinister black locusts, sending up the dust devils on that long abandoned runway and sweeping the long summer grass back and forth in rippling green waves. Up in his hiding place, the Peeper snapped shot after shot, although he knew the definition was poor. The Russians always paid well for photos which revealed SAS tactics; they feared that one day they might well be used against them behind the Warsaw Pact lines. Boris, his contact at their London Embassy, had once brought him a whole jar of Beluga caviare and a case of pink Crimean Champagne after he had supplied him with a photo of a SAS tactical heli-attack.

He ducked suddenly as the fleet of choppers swept over his hiding place, whipping the bracken to and fro; then they were gone, heading south. Within minutes they were just black dots on the leaden August sky.

Cautiously he raised himself and focused his camera for a last time. The five civilians, one of them definitely some kind of a darkie, were now lined up on the abandoned runway, waiting for the black Mercedes which was heading towards them over the rough tarmac. Now they were clearly outlined. The Peeper's tongue slipped out of the side of his slack wet lips, another dewdrop hanging from his nose. One by one, he took a mug-shot of them. He'd deliver it to the Yanks to run through their information banks. With whatever they found out, he'd go to Boris and hit him for a few quid, and then – he frowned at the thought – he'd go to the Chief of Staff.

God, what a bastard that man was. An Englishman to boot, but more Irish than some country-born Paddy from the bogs. Yet the Peeper knew that no one crossed the Chief of Staff and survived. He would have you knee-capped at the drop of a hat. He shivered at the memory of the day he had seen them deal with the 'grass', holding him down, while one of the boys calmly shot him through each knee-cap, sending a welter of bright red gore and gleaming broken bone spurting upwards and crippling the poor sod for life.

'Holy Mother of Jasus!' he cried out in sudden fear, his face contorted. 'Give me some real dough soon. Holy Mary, I'm just a poor old no-good gay with an ugly mug and bad breath. Not important to nobody. Let me out of this before they knee-cap me as well! Give me money and let me go to California, *please*!'

Carried away by sudden unreasoning fear, the Peeper flung a look at the sky, his free hand raised in a gesture of supplication, as if he half-expected to see his prayers answered by some magic of that Catholic faith to which, as a boy, he had desired to belong so desperately. But the grey August sky over Yorkshire was empty of any portents save the white contrails of the jets flying routine patrols, waiting for that day of blood that would come sooner or later.

When he looked at the abandoned airfield again, the five civilians had gone. The Peeper sighed. Wearily, he started to pack away his Jap camera. With luck he'd make the five o'clock King's Cross train out of York, and hit the seven o'clock *treff* with Boris at the gay pub just off Shaftesbury Avenue that he frequented. Suddenly the Peeper's face brightened. Perhaps Rock would be there, too. He was always game for a little naked wrestling and rough horseplay in return for a few quid. And how deliciously sweaty he always smelled afterwards!

A few minutes later he was on his way, trudging down the little country road, bearing with him the photos that could mean death for the Special Boat Service's Alpha Team...

BOOK TWO

The Big Snatch

'Often most valuable clues can be picked up by spies who get beneath windows and peer in at the corners at critical times.'

William Le Queux

1

'Leaving Turkish air space now, sir!' the pilot called. Behind him, sealed inside his space suit and strapped into a rocket-powered ejection seat with stainless steel cables latched to his boots, Top answered, 'Roger that, Major,' and tensed.

Only ten minutes earlier, the Blackbird had started from Izmir Field on the southern coast of Turkey, its after-burners thrusting the ship, the size of a Boeing 727 but with space for only two passengers, forward as if out of a cannon. Within three minutes they had levelled out at 25,000 feet, and the big, grey-haired civilian behind the pilot, known universally as 'Top Kick' or 'Top' – for that is what he had once been – had started to breathe again. Now they were actually out over the Black Sea, heading for Russia, sitting in tandem behind the spy plane's triangular cock-pit windows, which gleamed like evil, slanting eyes above the plane's sinister black tapered nose.

'Our flight path, sir, is set by a computer

that tracks fifty-two stars, twenty-four hours a day, sir,' the pilot's voice informed him, as they flew steadily northwards. 'The computer is accurate enough to guide the SR⋆ to any target on earth with an error of less than one thousand feet.'

'Bully for the SR,' Top sneered. He had recovered a little now, reverting to his usual tough, no-nonsense self. 'But answer me two questions.'

'Sir?'

'Can the Commies bounce us with their MIGs or whatever they're flying over the Black Sea area?'

'No sir,' the major answered promptly. 'Although the SR was first built twenty years ago, it is the highest-flying aircraft in the world and holds both world speed and altitude records. To be exact 2,193 *mph* in level flight at 85,000 feet. No MIG can reach us at that altitude, sir.'

'Roger that,' the big ex-noncom said with relief, his beefy face behind the mask flushed with heat and a lifetime of bellying up to bars for his daily intake of 'suds'. 'Next question. What kind of visual are we gonna get once we hit Commie air space?'

⋆ The Lockheed SR-71

'Perfect,' the pilot answered without the slightest hesitation.

'How do you mean, perfect?' Top snapped a little angrily. In all his thirty years of service for the 'good ole US of A', as he liked to call his country, he had never been able to hide his contempt for these classy Air Force hotshots. He guessed he was still the same old grunt he had been as the youngest Top Shirt in the Big Red One.★ 'Nuthin's *perfect*.'

'The SR is, sir. We carry high-resolution cameras as well as imaging radar that can take pictures in the dark and through cloud. We also possess sensors that can look sideways. So if necessary, we can fly outside Russian air space and peer deep into the interior. That way we can map one hundred thousand square miles of territory in one hour. At eighty thousand feet, the horizon is four hundred miles away and we can see the curvature of the earth, so that we have almost an unlimited view. At the same time—'

'Okay, okay!' growled Top, 'I'm convinced. Does this thing fuck as well?'

★The United States' premier infantry division, the First Infantry

75

The major didn't respond. Top's craggy face, marred by the scars of three decades of bar-room brawls and battle, broke into a grin. These Air Force jocks had no sense of humour. 'Okay, I didn't mean it. What's the deal?'

'As soon as we start to approach Soviet airspace, sir, I shall put the SR into a long, curving ballistic descent. By the way, don't touch the canopy, even with your gloves. It'll be blisteringly hot – six hundred degrees Fahrenheit, to be exact.'

'Hell, that's as hot as a domestic oven!' Top exclaimed, impressed in spite of himself.

'*Twice* as hot!' the pilot corrected him. 'It'll be supersonic all the way until I level out at thirty thousand feet. That should give the cameras the optimal position for photography.'

'Will they get the ship?'

'Naturally, sir.'

'Naturally my ass!' Top sneered ironically. But now the major was no longer listening as the spy plane vaulted forward at Mach Three, with the indicator clicking off the miles – more than one every two seconds. At more than 2,100 *mph*, the SR71 was racing over the water, the heavens above as black as outer space, faster than the muzzle velocity of a rifle bullet.

Ed Gilmour, known in US clandestine circles from Vietnam to Venezuela as 'Top', tried to forget that yellow ring between his legs. If he were forced to pull it in the event of an 'abort', the stainless steel cables would snap his legs back instantly, the canopy would blow open, and he would be shot 400 feet straight upwards, ejected right into the Commies' hands! Instead he tried to concentrate on the problem on hand.

When they had handed him the assignment, back at Langley, the desk chief had called it a 'lulu', a 'real ole sonuvabitch'. But Top, who had been engaged in covert ops ever since Korea, had reduced it, as always, to the essentials. For the time being, there were two things to be established. First, was the Commie pleasure cruiser, the SS *Varna*, actually anchored off the coast. Secondly, was anything unusual happening in or around the Bulgarian Communist Party holiday camp 'Praha', reserved for the Eastern European 'wheels', at the little Black Sea resort town of Byala?

Any sign of unusual activity – patrol boats out to sea where there hadn't been any before; naval craft engaged in 'exercises' near the SS *Varna*; more than usual auto-mobile activity on the exit roads from Byala – and they were in trouble. The big snatch would have to be called off.

'Big snatch,' he muttered to himself, and leered. *'The biggest snatch in history,'* the newspaper headlines would call it in due course. That would get a big horse-laugh from the guys at Langley. There'd be a lot of knowing looks and nudges, plus some pretty snide remarks about what Miss Johns had to offer below the plimsoll line. Top's leer changed to a frown. Typical of those smart-ass college graduates at Langley. *They* weren't laying it on the line in Moscow like Miss Johns. If things went wrong next week, it wouldn't be *their* asses that were in the sling. No sir! He shook his head in admiration. In spite of her profession, in his book, Miss Johns, was a number one Joe.

'Sir,' the pilot's voice cut into his reverie. 'To port. It must be the SS *Varna*. The computers never lie.'

'In a pig's ass!' Top growled and craned his neck forward, eyes narrowed beneath the black face mask. Set against a sweep of perfect blue, there was a tiny black dot. He checked to left and right and beyond to the brown smudge which was Russia. Nothing!

Not even the white wakes of pleasure boats. There *seemed* to be nothing unusual going on around the pleasure cruiser. 'Can you take her down a little – safely?' he asked hesitantly.

'Sure,' the major answered confidently. 'I'll do a dipsy-doodle and buzz her at thirty thousand.'

'Dipsy-doodle?' Top snorted, angry as always when he heard a new piece of jargon. These days it seemed that the whole goddam world conspired to bamboozle him with new words. Christ, nobody spoke good ole plain American any more! 'What in Sam Hill's that?'

'SOP, sir.* We climb to 33,000 feet and then dip down to 30,000. That gets us through the sound barrier quickly and more efficiently. You won't even hear the boom when we slide through Mach One.'

'Let's hope the Commies won't either,' Top growled.

'Don't worry about that, sir. The opposition will already have registered our presence here, I'm sure. But they don't have any military interceptors that can exceed Mach Two. And they can fly at that speed

*Standard operating procedure

79

for only short periods, because Mach Two speeds eat up most of their fuel. Blackbird here can cruise in excess of Mach Three for extended periods.'

The pride in the pilot's voice was obvious, but Top was unimpressed. Indeed, he had made it part of his make-up *never* to appear impressed. It gave a lot of smart dudes wrong ideas. So he said, 'Okay, Major, let's get on the stick. I got some ice-cold suds waiting for me back at the officers' club at Izmir and it's way past my personal happy hour already. Let's go.'

At 1000 *mph* they zipped over the pleasure cruiser. For an instant it was there, and then it was gone, left far behind them on that vast blue glittering sea, and they were circling over the Bulgarian coast, their cameras clicking away madly as they photographed every possible exit road from the remote little coastal resort, reserved solely for high-ranking Communist Party officials from the Eastern bloc.

Now the cockpit was beginning to fill with the odour of burnt metal, as the titanium alloy of which the plane was constructed began to heat up to 600 degrees. Top looked nervously to left and right to check whether the engines were on fire.

'Don't worry,' the pilot's calm voice came over the intercom, 'it smells like that every time.'

'I'm not worrying,' Top snorted indignantly. 'With a hotshot pilot like you–' He stopped short, his indignation vanished. 'Hey, what's that? At three o'clock.'

'Visitors,' the pilot replied immediately, his voice no longer so calm.

'You mean Commie interceptors?' Top cried, as the black dots grew larger and larger at an alarming rate.

'Yes, sir. But don't worry. I flew this baby over Hanoi for a year and the Russians had set up a laboratory of their best anti-aircraft guns and radar there. They couldn't touch–' His voice broke off abruptly.

'What is it?'

'Look, sir.'

Brazen lights were beginning to blink off and on in the enemy planes.

Top recognised them at once. *'Jesus H!'* he cried. 'Them's fuckin' missiles, and the mothers are heading for us... *And this ain't fuckin' Hanoi!'* He swallowed hard as a thin white line started to streak across the bright blue of the sky. 'Let's beat it!'

'Taking evasive action now, sir,' the major cried crisply, as the missile streaked by below them and then began to circle as it commenced its search for the heat of the jet's twin engines.

'Roger that!' Top called, as the Blackbird leapt upwards and the missile fell behind, vanishing in seconds. He took one last look at the land before it disappeared into the blackness. He'd be back – but next time, he'd hike it like the darned good infantry-man he had once been. There'd be no more Fancy-Dan spy planes for ole Top!

Ten minutes later they had started down on that long, curving ballistic descent which would bring them to Izmir Field, and the big grey ex-noncom had convinced himself it would work. *Operation Bluebeard had commenced...*

2

Aft, the Turkish skipper flicked on the fishing boat's big overhanging lantern, once, twice, three times, and then turned it off as if he were having difficulty with it. Top nodded his approval and pulled the sweater over his grey, crew-cut head. He shivered a little in the night breeze, heavy with the scent of resin and wild herbs, wafting out to sea from the Bulgarian shore. Miss Johns couldn't have missed that signal, and any other observer would have taken it for a fishing boat setting up for a night's fishing.

The Turk came ambling barefoot towards the waiting American, followed by his sons, who acted as crew. They all smelled of sweat, fish, garlic and yoghourt. Top could have detected that they were Turks by the smell alone half a mile away. All the Turks he knew seemed to smell like that, but for his book, the Turks weren't bad Joes – and they hated the Commies like poison.

'*Raki lutfen!*' the skipper commanded, and clapped his hands in the Turkish fashion.

One of his sons slipped away to the little cabin to fetch the drink.

The skipper smiled at Top, who was busy fixing the waterproof bag which contained his gear and clothing, gold teeth glittering in the glowing darkness. 'Good, eh?' He indicated the silver crescent moon sailing above the still sea. 'Moon good.'

'Yep,' Top agreed, finishing the preparations for his swim, and even ventured a few words of Turkish, feeling a little foolish as he always did when he wasn't speaking good ole plain American. *'Cok gusel.'* The Turks had a funny thing about the moon. They were always looking up at it and letting off goddam long sighs. Must be something to do with their religion, he concluded, and strapped the bag to the leather belt tied around his waist.

The barefoot boy reappeared with a little tray bearing two glasses of raki and a bottle of cheap lemon eau-de-cologne. 'Drink,' the skipper urged, and handed Top a glass of fiery spirits. 'Death to Russian pigs!' he said fervently.

'Sure,' Top agreed, and drained the glass in one go. He felt the alcohol thump his guts with a red-hot punch. A warm glow surged through his big, naked body immediately.

Awkwardly, he dragged his bag to the side of the little caique. Half a mile away the lights of Byala blazed away merrily, and he thought he could just make out snatches of fast accordion music. 'They sure do have a long happy hour in this neck of the woods,' he whispered to himself. It was almost eleven at night. But it was all to the good. By this time the Commies had to be bombed out of their skulls.

Behind him, the skipper ordered one of his sons to pour the cheap cologne over his calloused dirty hands before stretching his right out in parting. 'Allah go with you!' he declared.

Top took the hand gingerly, glad that it had been partially disinfected by the cologne. Montezuma's Revenge was epidemic in Turkey, and he didn't want to catch a dose of the shits at this stage of the game. 'Thanks, skipper,' he replied. 'Tell my guys back there that I reached the place safely, okay?'

'Okay,' the skipper said jauntily, liking the sound of the word. 'I okay him!'

Top nodded, concentrating exclusively on the task before him and hoping that the briefing officer, another one of those young hotshots from Harvard, had been right

85

about the speed and direction of the tide off Byala. Carefully he slipped on his big rubber flippers and edged himself over the side. The water was warm, as he had been promised. Next moment the buoyant, watertight bag dropped next to him. He was in.

Behind him, the skipper called something in Turkish, but Top was no longer listening. His whole attention was fixed on the shore some half a mile away; for now, he knew, although he belonged to the most powerful secret organisation of the most powerful nation on the earth, he was completely on his own. He started to swim...

Top was an old-style American. In the days before Vietnam, his type could have been seen on every US military base: big, heavy, shaven-headed and confident. In those days, the bar of every NCO club right across the world from Bragg to Berlin was full of them – men who had served their country well and believed that nowhere was there a better place on this earth than the 'ZI'* or the 'land of the round doorknob', as they called it in their own military slang.

For them, foreigners were 'gooks' and

*Zone of the Interior, *i.e.* the United States

86

'slopeheads', 'apeshits' and 'Spic smack-heads'. The enemy were 'Commie dinks', and anybody who didn't believe in the 'good ole US of A' were obviously 'fags' and 'fruits', if not downright 'treacherous shit-heels'.

They believed in the 'raising the flag at Iwo Jima', and MacAuliffe telling the Krauts 'nuts' at Bastogne. Tears came into their bloodshot eyes when the band played *The Yellow Rose of Texas* and they were ever fond of declaring drunkenly, 'Shit, I may be old-fashioned, but I'm an American, and there ain't nothing wrong with that, is there, mister?' It was a question that warranted no answer, especially if the speaker had a fist like a small steam shovel.

'Nam', 'Kent State', 'Flower Power', 'Watergate' and all the rest of that dreary litany of 'darned betrayal,' as they saw it, had changed everything for men like Top. Now they were desperate men, out of step with their time, way out on a limb, fighting 'dirty' in order to preserve what was left of America's heritage.

For Top and a lot of the old-timers like him, who had grown grey and old in the service of their country, clandestine ops, however messy, offered a last chance to get back at those 'Commie dinks' who had nearly ruined the 'ZI'. They didn't serve 'Uncle Sugar' for the dough, like so many of the 'smartass dudes' who now filled the ranks of the CIA and the other intelligence-gathering agencies; they weren't even in it for a pension, free medical treatment and Class Six privileges, as a lot of the new-type 'head shirts'.* They were in it because they *believed*. 'We're a goddam dying breed,' Top and his kind would declare drunkenly in their bars, which were invariably decorated with a large poster of John Wayne. 'But by Christ, we're gonna go out fighting!'

Thus it was that Ed Gilmour, alias Top, found himself swimming the Black Sea towards the coast of Bulgaria at the age of fifty-five, knowing that if he were caught, the Commies would give him the old 'sweetsour' treatment in that notorious fourth-floor jail in Moscow's Lubianka, and no doubt in the end, a 9mm slug to the base of the skull in some discreet basement one early morning. He was risking his life at an age when he should have been sitting on the porch with his feet up, drinking his Schlitz beer, because he *believed*...

*Senior NCOs.

He could smell her first, as he staggered out of the light surf, tugging the bag awkwardly after him. There was no mistaking that perfume. It was pure America: a compound of deodorant, toilet soap, and American class. Taking no chances all the same, he pulled the little silenced pistol out of the bag and crouching there in the stunted pines that lined the shore, he called softly, *'Miss Johns … Miss Jo-Jo Johns?'*

'Mister Gilmour, Edward Gilmour?' she queried, with equal formality for two agents who were risking death in the midst of the enemy camp.

'Yes, it's me, Top.' He rose to his full height and watched her shadow detach itself from the trees and heard the soft rustle of silk.

She came to him with her hand outstretched. 'Good to see you, Top. Heard a lot about ya from the crowd at the Moscow Embassy. They say you're a number one guy.'

Top felt himself colouring, and only in part from the praise. It wasn't every day that a guy of his age stood close to such a beautiful woman in the dark, naked as he was save for a pair of swimming shorts. 'Everything okay?' he whispered urgently, as he started to pull his clothes from the bag.

'Sure,' she said easily. 'The whole bunch of them, all the top brass, are getting loaded on that cheap Bulgarian brandy of theirs in the House of Culture. They should be well and truly stoned by now, including friend Bluebeard – the big chauvinistic Commie pig!' She gave a soft silvery laugh, and Top's heart went right out to her. It was a god-awful shame that such a classy dame had to let a jerk like that get his rocks off on her.

'Has he been behaving himself, Miss Johns?' he asked, drying himself swiftly with the towel.

'Sure. As tame as a little lamb when he's not stoned. And by the way, Top, call me Jo-Jo.'

'Okay, sure, er, Jo-Jo.' Suddenly Top felt oddly embarrassed. 'I wonder if you'd ... turn the other way?' he asked hesitantly. 'Got to take my – er, shorts off.'

She gave that light, silvery laugh of hers that reminded him of some gal in one of those big houses in the antebellum Deep South back in the days when Hollywood made *real* movies; but she turned obediently enough.

Hurriedly he slipped on his jockey shorts and pulled his slacks on after them. A minute later he was dressed. 'All right now, Jo-Jo.'

She turned and pressed his hand spontaneously. 'You're a funny guy, Top. But I like you. Too many guys these days are ready to sock it to you even before they say hi.'

Top's jaw hardened. 'Yeah, I know just what you mean,' he said, realising just what she must have suffered. Then he got down to business. 'Right, Jo-Jo, this is the deal. The SS *Varna* picks up the tourists – they're mostly Krauts from West Germany – from the coast tomorrow afternoon. It sails on the evening tide. Next port of call, Istanbul. From there, Alexandria, Egypt, and then on to Marseilles, France.'

'Do we leave it there?' she asked quickly, as a door was flung open a hundred yards away and a singing man stumbled out into the night and started to urinate.

Watching, Top frowned; they ought to castrate guys who took leaks in front of ladies like that. 'No, you can't trust the Frogs. Half of them are Commies anyway. No, we stick with the ship till it reaches the Bay of Rosas up in northern Spain. On the Med, near the Spics' frontier with the Frogs.'

Over the way, the drunken man had interrupted his song to break wind loudly. Top clenched his fist and hoped that Miss Jo-Jo hadn't heard. What kind of crap-heels were these chickenshit Commie dinks, ripping off a fart like that!

Hurriedly he continued as the man staggered back inside again, a loud burst of fast accordion-and-fiddle music hitting the night air as he opened the door to the House of Culture. 'We go ashore on a day excursion there. Our people from Zaragossa Air Base will be waiting for us. They'll fly us to Rhine-Main, and from there we take him to Oberursel.'

'The Interrogation Centre?'

In the light from the open door Top saw her face for the first time, framed by that silver-blonde hair. His heart missed a beat. She was beautiful – like a kind of sexier Doris Day before she dropped Rock Hudson and got mean. 'Yeah. Prelim debriefing. We just want to be sure that he ain't handing us a bum steer. Then from Rhine-Main straight to Dulles, Washington.'

She absorbed the information, and he could almost hear her brain working as she followed the itinerary of the bold escape plan.

'You see, Jo-Jo, the deal is to keep him under cover for as long as possible before the KGB gooks figure out what's happened. That's why we suggested this vacation way out here in the boonies so far away from Moscow, with loused-up communications. We don't want their Directorate S alerting their illegals and other agents before we get to them.* This guy Bluebeard has cost the good ole US of A a heap of dough – not to mention your personal effort…' He cleared his throat with sudden embarrassment.

'You can say that again, Top. Christ, do you know that jerk only changes his socks once a month? And that's only for openers.'

Top thought it was not opportune to enquire any further on that score. Instead he said hurriedly, 'State and Langley want to squeeze him dry, Jo-Jo, till the pips begin to squeak.'

She nodded her agreement. 'Roger,' she said. 'But what about the heavies?'

'The heavies?'

'Yes. He's got a couple of bodyguards. I call them 'Fat' and 'Thin' – that's the Russki name for Laurel and Hardy. They're built that way, you see: one small and lean, the other, big and fat. But they're both very mean hombres. You know – the kind of guys

*Ultra-secret KGB organisation which runs Soviet citizens working under deep cover in foreign countries

93

who pull the legs off bugs. And they don't even drink when they're on duty.' She jerked her thumb at the House of Culture. 'They'll be in there now, watching Yuri – er, Bluebeard – with their beady eyes, not letting him out of their sight for a minute.'

Top grinned suddenly as he thought of the plan they had worked out at Izmir for the two bodyguards. 'Jo-Jo, it's all taken care of. My honcho is so thorough that if a Commie dink burps, he'll know what key the guy burps in.'

She gave one of those delightful laughs of hers and clutched his arm momentarily. Top's nostrils were assailed by the wonderful smell of her and the feel of that soft, nubile body. For an instant Top wished he was young again; that he wasn't twenty-five pounds overweight and hadn't lost his teeth when the NVA had shelled the base on that last horrific day at Tan Son Nhut before the chickenshit yellow slopeheads had run the goddam US Army out of Nam for good.

'How do you mean, Top?' she asked. 'What's your plan?'

'Ex-lax,' he answered simply.

'*Ex-lax*?'

'Sure. The most powerful laxative those smart dudes in the labs at Langley could come up with. It's supposed to make Montezuma's Revenge look like a hot flush. Excuse my French, Jo-Jo,' he added hastily, blushing in the darkness.

'No sweat, Top. Go on.'

'Well, you know the kind of chow these gooks around here eat? Yoghourt, unwashed peppers, tomatoes, okra and that kind of stuff. It'd blow a hole in anybody's stomach. So we feed them the Ex-lax. It should keep them in the – excuse me, in the latrines for the next forty-eight hours... And by then, me, you and Bluebeard will be long, long gone...'

3

'*Boshe moi!*' Bluebeard chortled, as they raced down the dusty Bulgarian coastal road towards the frontier, his moonlike face streaming with sweat that glistened in bright pearls on the top of his shaven skull. 'You hear noise from shithouse? Like atomic bombs exploding!' He took his fat paws off the wheel of the Wartburg, and puffing out his plump cheeks, gave a tremendous Bronx cheer, the veins standing out purple at his temples. '*Boom... Boom... Boom! Horoscho...* Good, eh, American?'

Top sat hunched in the back of the little East German automobile, his big hand clutching his pistol. He grunted something and frowned. He didn't like that kind of talk in front of a lady. In the USA you didn't talk about the 'bathroom' like that. But Jo-Jo didn't seem to mind. Sitting next to the Russian giant, she looked as cool as ice in her blue silk dress, her beautiful face set in a smile, almost as if she was actually enjoying the Commie dink's dirty talk.

So far it had all gone amazingly well. Blue-beard had managed to slip the dope into the raspberry tea with syrup that the dinks drank for breakfast, and half an hour later it had all started. The two bodyguards had been rolling about their bunks in agony, clutching their guts and ripping off tremen-dous farts as if their arses might explode at any moment. For the record, Bluebeard had called the holiday camp's doctor, who had appeared, unshaven and hung-over, with a bandage soaked in vinegar around his aching forehead. 'Shits,' he had diagnosed routinely, according to Bluebeard's trans-lation, 'Black Sea shits!' Giving a handful of pills to the two writhing, moaning men, their hard faces almost green in colour now, he had then staggered over to the beach bar – which was already serving iced beer and plum brandy, even though it was only nine o'clock in the morning. Thereafter the two sorely stricken bodyguards had taken up residence in the primitive, iron-roofed beach latrines, which stank to high heaven, their roofs rippling in the burning blue waves of the new day's heat.

An hour later they had been on their way. Telling the camp guards that they were off on a day's sight-seeing in the surrounding

Bulgarian countryside, they set off in the squat East German Wartburg with Top hidden in the boot. As soon as they were clear of the place, Top had climbed out, his shirt wet with sweat, and together he and the big Russian spymaster had changed over the Russian plates to the East German ones that Top had brought with him from Turkey. Now they were three East German Party officials on holiday in Bulgaria, driving along the country roads that skirted the Gulf of Burgas, the only traffic consisting of lumbering ox-drawn farm carts, piled high with maize, and the occasional East German mopeds, driven by proud, black-eyed, barefoot peasant boys. By midday – the timing was important – they would be at the frontier.

'Boris and Vladimir,' Bluebeard roared uproariously, as he belted along the blindingly white country road, 'forget me now. Problem with guts. By time find out, Yuri in Disneyland, North America, with beautiful Jo-Jo, *nitchivo*?' Possessively he pressed his big fingers, thick as pork sausages, deep into Jo-Jo's nylon-clad knee and gave Top a big, gold-toothed grin in the rearview mirror, winkingly knowingly, as he did so. 'Amerikanski Dollar, too!'

Top frowned. It wasn't right for these hairy-assed Commie dinks to get their blue-veiners with honest-to-goodness American gals. Let them screw their own kind, with asses on 'em like ten-dollar Missouri mules. For a moment he visualised the two of them in bed: the gross Russian giant with his startlingly red sensualist's lips, and the petite but well-built Jo-Jo. God, what kind of suffering she must have had to go through with the Commie smackhead! Did he make her do *that* to his diamond-cutter? Christ on a crutch, not go down on him? Inwardly he groaned and hastily dismissed the horrifying vision and concentrated on the task in hand, as the Wartburg hurtled through a village, tearing up a thick wake of white dust and scattering squawking chickens in front of it, with the sweating Russian laughing madly at the wheel.

Their East German ID was perfect. Everything right, bang up-to-date, signed and sealed in Pankow two weeks before.* Their West German passports, which they were to use to board the *Varna*, were one hundred percent in order as well. They even bore the correct Russian entry visa stamps

*East German Party HQ

to show that they had entered Russia one week before with the rest of the tour, to spend several days sunning themselves on the Black Sea coast before returning on board to complete the second half of the cruise. According to Intelligence, the Commies never bothered West German tourists much anyway; they provided too valuable a source of foreign currency with their vaunted 'hard D-Mark'.

As Top saw it, there were two real problems. A body search would reveal the five thousand in Dollars and ten thousand in Marks that each of them carried, plus the little West German pistol. Probably they could talk their way out of it by saying they didn't know there was a Soviet law against the illegal importation of foreign currency and weapons. But the real problem might start if whoever stopped them could speak Kraut or brought up an official interpreter. Then the shit would really hit the fan. For although all three of them had enough German to fool the average cop or official, any fluent native speaker would recognise them as non-Germans within moments. The trick then was to cross the border and the strip of Russian territory to the waiting SS *Varna* as quickly as possible. If they were stopped, palms would have to be greased.

Bluebeard ripped the car round a bend on two wheels, laughing uproariously as a peasant woman crouching in a ditch screamed and flung down her wide skirts to hide her broad naked bottom. 'Bulgaria,' he yelled, 'all shit!' His thick hairy fingers dug ever deeper into Jo-Jo's delightful knee.

'Yuri!' Top cried above the roar of the engine. 'Take it easy, willya? Or you'll never live to collect that fat pension Washington's promised ya!'

'*Kak shal*!' Bluebeard said sadly, but he took his foot off the accelerator a little and the Wartburg slowed down to 70 *mph*. He set his face in a sulky little boy's look.

'Thanks,' Top said with a sigh. There seemed to be only two kinds of Commie dinks: morose, silent and suspicious, or loud, raucous and crazy. Bluebeard seemed to be one of the second kind, like an overgrown kid. Yet Top suspected there was tough, ice-cold hardness underneath all that jolly laughing blubber. There *had* to be for a dink to claw himself up right to the top of the KGB, as Bluebeard had done in these last twenty years. Top wasn't an imaginative man; he had nothing but contempt for 'shrinks' and similar 'feather merchants' –

but somehow he sensed that Yuri Serov wasn't all he appeared to be. For an instant an icy finger trailed its way down his spine. What if those smart dudes back in Langley were wrong? It wouldn't be the first time that those fink desk jockeys had made a mistake and some poor shit out in the field had gotten his ass burned as a result... He shivered involuntarily.

'What matter, Top?' Bluebeard asked. 'Louse run over liver, eh?'

Top shook his head angrily. 'Ner,' he growled. 'Now get a load of this, Yuri, and you, too, Miss Johns.'

'Sure, Top,' she said, and with practised ease removed Bluebeard's fingers from her knee before they could start their climb up the nylon to those delightful secret places. 'Knock it, off, Yuri! It's too goddam hot for that kinda stuff.'

Top flushed and said hastily, 'In thirty minutes we should be at the frontier. According to my info, it's guarded not by the usual Soviet border police, but by militiamen. That's why Langley chose it.'

Bluebeard hawked dramatically and spat lazily out of the window. 'Militiamen ... *Pigs,*' he said contemptuously. 'No good pigs. Always this.' With his free paw he made the Russian gesture of counting money. 'Nobody like militia. Do anything for money. Even murder.'

'So I've heard, Yuri.'

'They hate us of the KGB.' He spat again. 'I shit on them, pigs.' His false teeth bulged from his red lips. 'Hooligans!'

Top flushed. The big dink would open his mouth even in a shit storm! He had no idea of how to behave in the presence of a lady. Hastily he went on. 'The trick is to get through fast. Don't talk much – and not a word in English. Just Kraut. Remember our cover.' He looked warningly. 'No rough stuff. Even if they seem to be about to give us flak, leave it to me.' He pulled the green East German passport out of his pocket where it lay next to the pistol and opened it next to the blue star of the stencilled Bulgarian entry visa. A fifty-Dollar note, crisp and new, lay there neatly. 'Fifty bucks. Big money in this neck of the woods. If the militia are everything you and Intelligence say they are, Yuri, it should be as easy as falling off a log.'

'*Horoscho*!' Bluebeard said, nodding his head in agreement. 'That is it... Money militia understand ... Always. *Da, da.*'

Top flashed Jo-Jo a quick glance. She

smiled as sweetly as ever, as if she had total confidence in what the two men had just said. But there was a wary, taut look in her blue eyes, and her hands lying on her lap had suddenly tensed. Top realised that she was scared and his heart went out to her. At that moment he promised himself that nothing, but nothing, would happen to Jo-Jo, come what may...

The militiamen sweated in the heat, lounging in the shade of the parched trees, collars ripped open, caps pushed to the back of their heads, rifles slung carelessly over their shoulders. A single man guarded the red-and-white-striped pole which barred the little road, eyeing the Bulgarian guards a hundred yards off malevolently, as if they were deadly enemies instead of socialist brothers-in-arms. All was heavy silence broken only by the sound of their own car engine, crawling along noisily through no-man's land in first gear.

Top, in his time, had crossed a dozen borders or more illegally, but he had never gotten used to it. His lips were parched, his heart was racing frantically, and the tips of his fingers were sweaty and trembling with tension as he touched the butt of the pistol, now taped to the inside of his thigh. Even Jo-Jo, who had carefully raised the hem of her skirt to show as much shapely leg as possible and distract the guards' attention, was suddenly flushed and nervous. Only Bluebeard, the man who had most to lose, seemed absolutely calm. He braked carefully and slumped back in his seat, waiting for the militiamen to come forward.

A skinny-ribbed dog raised itself with an effort from the dirty gutter, staggered to the edge of the frontier post and urinated lazily, before collapsing in the dust again, tongue hanging out, as if completely exhausted by the sweltering heat.

Slowly, very slowly, the man slumped over the barrier raised himself. He stared at the car's plates as if having difficulty focusing his eyes in this baking heat. Then he called to no one in particular, *'Nmetski.'*

Near the post, another militiaman shoved his cap down and, unslinging his rifle, advanced on them with infinite weariness, as if it caused him tremendous pain simply to drag one leg after another. He came level with Bluebeard. He held out a grubby hand that smelled of sweat and garlic, the middle finger bent inwards, as if he were about to tickle something, *'Papiere,'* he said.

Top's heart skipped a beat. *The dink spoke Kraut!*

Bluebeard never stopped smiling, and there was something contemptuous in his smile, as if he had already assessed the dirty, slow militiaman and his assessment wasn't a favourable one. He turned slowly and accepted Top's and Jo-Jo's passports, placing Top's, with its fifty-Dollar bill, on top.

Taking his time, ignoring the fly crawling over his sweaty, dark face, the militiaman accepted them and began to leaf through Top's passport with that typical indolent contempt of border police the world over, occasionally grunting something over his shoulder to the frontier hut with its blacked-out windows.

Top felt a cold trickle of sweat run down the small of his back, and his clothes started to stick to him unpleasantly. He knew the drill of old. All the Commie countries practised it. In the box there would be a superior officer, never seen by the public, who kept in front of him the local blacklists of all wanted people. At his elbow would be the telephone which linked him to the nearest office of state security. Unknown to the nervous traveller, he was the one who decided if they should proceed or not, be shadowed afterwards, and possibly, later, 'lose' his passport – assuming it could be used by Commie agents in due course. The minutes ticked away leadenly. Top's fingers thrust through the hole in his trousers' pocket and curled round the damp butt of the pistol taped to his thigh.

Suddenly the lazy-eyed militiaman came to the page with the crisp, new fifty-Dollar bill. His tiredness vanished abruptly. He looked hard at Bluebeard.

Top flashed a glance at Bluebeard's face reflected in the rear-view mirror. The fat Commie dink's eyes flashed fire. They radiated power – and command. For a fleeting second the militiaman stiffened, as if he might well spring to attention – but only for a second. Next instant he was his lazy, careless self, as he deftly palmed the bill and thrust the passports, the other two unchecked, into Bluebeard's fat paw.

'*Davai*!' the militiaman commanded and, raising the striped pole, waved them on. '*Davai!*'

Bluebeard didn't hesitate. He thrust home first gear and, letting out the clutch, began to move forward. They were inside the Soviet Union!

Behind them the militiaman let the pole down noisily and slumped over it, as if the effort in that terrible heat had exhausted him. Lazily the skinny-ribbed dog came limping across through the dust and began to urinate once more – on his boot. The militiaman didn't seem to notice.

4

The two cops appeared as if from nowhere. One moment the road leading down to the Black Sea and the SS *Varna* was empty – the usual blinding-white stretch of dusty track; the next moment, there they were: two big, burly men, clad in thigh-length leather jackets in spite of the heat, faces beneath the peaked caps half-hidden by dark goggles, with their gloved hands resting significantly on their pistol holsters.

Bluebeard cursed in Russian and started to slow down obediently, as one raised his free hand, bearing in it a small round metal disk. With a sinking heart, Top knew, it was the signal to halt.

Jo-Jo flashed him a frightened look. 'Why are they stopping us, Top?' she hissed, as Bluebeard, his fat face very serious now, made a noisy mess of changing down from top to third. 'We're nearly at the boat now.' She indicated the shimmering blue sea and the brilliant white shape of the cruise ship, poised on it like a child's toy boat on a pond.

'Don't worry, Miss Johns,' Top said with more confidence than he felt. 'We'll take care of it. They could well be just the same ole' traffic cops we have back in the States, out to make a pinch to kill a boring afternoon.'

'*Nyet!*' Bluebeard snarled, sweating heavily now, his fat face crimson, as they rolled ever closer to the two leather-clad giants in their top boots and baggy leather breeches. 'Here no automobiles. Why traffic cops?' He uttered an angry curse in Russian and changed down to second. They came to a stop.

Suddenly all was silent save the *throb-throb* of the Wartburg's engine and the sound of old-style dance music coming faintly across the water from the boat.

The cops let them wait. For what seemed an age they stared at each other, the fugitives and the police, frozen into immobility like cheap actors at the end of an even cheaper melodrama, just before the curtain goes down. Slowly, very slowly, Top began to click off his safety catch.

The bigger of the two brown-leather hulks was the first to move. Self-importantly, he bent to examine the front number plate, for what reason Top, sweating, anxious and tense, didn't know. He grunted. Behind him, his comrade kept his gauntleted hand on his pistol-butt. In spite of his nervousness, Top was ready to plug the guy in the gut if he had to. The belly presented a bigger target – and he would never make his trigger in time.

Ponderously, his heavy boots raising little clouds of white dust as he did so, the bigger one clanked to the back of the car. With an effort of sheer naked willpower, Top forced himself not to turn. Sweat started to pour in thick rivulets down the back of Bluebeard's shaven skull, and Top could see he was scared – shit scared. Across the water, the ship's band was playing *In the Mood* for all they were worth, as if Glenn Miller were still in the land of the living.

Behind them the cop grunted something. Top started. Bluebeard had stiffened visibly. There was no mistaking it. Something had gone wrong!

The cop to their front, sinister and somehow alien in his heavy leather gear and dark goggles, crooked a finger at them slowly.

Nobody moved.

Over on the ship, *In the Mood* had given way to a very laboured, almost burlesque version of *How Much Is That Doggie In the*

111

Window? At another time and another place, Top would have laughed out loud at such crap. Not now.

Angrily the smaller of the two motorcycle cops thrust up his goggles, to reveal an icy, light-pigmented nordic face, the kind of Swedish features that went with straight, honey-blond hair and that Top remembered from his Minnesota farming youth. *'Na, wird's bald?'* he demanded in perfect German. *'Ausweise, Autodokumerne, sonstige Papiere bereit halten... Los!'*

Top could have groaned out loud. They had run into a fluent German-speaker, perhaps from one of Russia's Baltic provinces! Just their rotten luck! Suddenly for no reason he could ever make out later, he remembered that old bitter song from Nam:

Fuck, fuck, luck this TBS shit,
Three more weeks and we'll be home,
Then it's off to Vietnam, lose a leg or lose an
  arm,
And be pensioned by the Corps for ever more!

He had always hated the self-indulgent defeatism of the chant the young grunts of the Marine Division had sung then, just as he hated now simply laying his head on the

112

block to be chopped off. A man didn't have to accept his fate like a goddam sheep being led to the slaughter; a *real* man fought back! Suddenly all fear and tension had vanished and he was complete master of the situation.

Pretending to fumble inside his jacket, he whispered urgently, 'Jo-Jo – out of your side of the vehicle. Shield us from the ship if you can. Yuri, you take the smaller one. I'll take the big jerk.'

Bluebeard opened his mouth as if to protest, but Top didn't give him a chance. 'No discussion,' he hissed. 'Perhaps they can see us from the *Varna*. Don't know but we're not taking any chances. We'll clobber them in the bushes. Okay, move it!'

Bluebeard was about to protest, but just then the taller policeman cried again in German, *'Los, Mensch! Raus!'*

'Move it!'

Watched closely by the cop in front and behind, the three of them left the car, Jo-Jo deliberately swinging her legs wide to distract the first policeman's attention momentarily. It worked. His eyes, blue, flinty and icy, widened as he caught a glimpse of those delicious thighs. For a second, he took his gaze off Top. It was fatal. Shielded from the man behind, Top ripped off the plaster and freed the pistol from his leg. Now it rested, hard, firm, and lethal in his hand, dug deep into his trouser pocket.

'*Na, nun wo sind Ihre Dokumente?*' the policeman demanded.

Top nudged Bluebeard and snatched out his passport to hand to the German-speaking cop.

The blond cop took it and flipped open the first page. Suddenly the suspicious look vanished from his face. '*Ah, ah,*' he cried, as if in triumph, '*ich war einmal in Rostock.*'

'Rostock?' Top stuttered, catching only the place name.

'*Ja, ja. Geboren Rostock steht hier. Ich war bei der Roten Flotte. Kennen Sie–*'

Hating to do this in front of Jo-Jo, Top grabbed the front of his pants dramatically and cried, '*Ich muss pissen ... Schnell!*' With a jerk of his head, he indicated the girl. '*Aber nicht vor der Dame, bitte...*'

The cop's animated look vanished. He looked puzzled and uncertain. For one terrible moment Top thought he was going to refuse his request, then the cop nodded in the direction of some parched, dusty bushes which lined the side of the little road.

Top beamed. In a flash he was in them, fumbling with his flies as he did so, as if he couldn't get there fast enough to urinate, to rip out the pistol and fit the little metal silencer. Behind him, the blond cop was still holding Top's passport and was now beginning to examine Bluebeard's, while Jo-Jo smiled madly.

Top nodded to her significantly.

She nodded back.

Top shot a look at the *Varna*. Her deck seemed empty. Perhaps the crew were below decks playing the corny old-fashioned music. Muttering a silent prayer that no one was watching through binoculars from the gleaming white bridge, he clutched the little pistol tightly to his side, then whipped round to face the group.

The other cop's mouth dropped open stupidly. Top could see that any moment he would shout a warning to the blond cop. He didn't give him a chance. He squeezed the trigger. A soft plop. The pistol jerked at his side. There was the sudden stink of burnt explosive. Suddenly the other cop's knees were buckling beneath him, his hands clawing the air furiously as if he were climbing the rungs of an invisible ladder, a patch of scarlet growing ever larger on the

115

chest of his leather tunic.

'*Duck, Jo-Jo!*' Top cried frantically. He couldn't risk firing at the blond cop with Jo-Jo directly behind him. 'Yuri, grab the bastard – *quick, man!*' He started to squeeze the trigger of the silenced pistol once more, hard jaw set, eyes glinting.

Jo-Jo hit the dust without hesitation, but Bluebeard, for some reason, didn't move. He remained rooted to the spot, his fat, moonlike face animated by a mixture of emotions that Top had no time to interpret at that tense moment.

'*For Chrissake!*' the big American snarled.

Suddenly the blond cop dropped the passports and in the very same instant sprang sidewards with the speed and agility of a ballet dancer, to come smashing into Top with heavy, studded boots. Next moment the two of them went slamming into the dust, the pistol tumbling from Top's hand with the shock of that surprise attack.

'*Verdammtes Schwein!*' the blond cop cried. Expertly he chopped his open hand upwards. The blow caught Top right at the base of his nose. A red wave of excruciating pain swept through his big frame. For a second he panicked and thought he was going to black out. '*Yuri,*' he called weakly.

116

'Get ... *the bastard*! ... I can't...' The rest of his words were choked as the cop's hands sought and found his throat and, immediately applied full pressure, the fingers digging cruelly into the soft flesh of Top's neck.

Desperately fighting off unconsciousness with the last of his strength, Top writhed back and forth, trying to break that vicelike grip. Twice he raised his knee. Both times the much younger cop easily dodged the blow to his testicles. Now he grunted dramatically, knowing that the big man trapped beneath him was fading fast. *'Die, bastard, die!'* he cried through gritted teeth in an ecstasy of bloodlust. *'Die!'*

But it wasn't to be. Suddenly a raging, shrieking fury descended upon the cop's broad back, one hand tugging at his long, sleek hair, the other wielding the dead cop's pistol, slamming its butt down and down, over and over again, until the man's yellow hair started to turn a startling, dramatic scarlet. With each blow the victim's broken-lunged voice grew weaker, pleading for mercy, while that shrill female harpy screamed, *'Let go of him, you lousy sonuva-bitch... Let go!'*

With a last grunt, Top scraped a little more parched soil over the shallow grave they had dug for the two dead cops with the shovel from the Wartburg and nodded to the Russian defector.

Wordlessly, his fat face set in that morose, dour look that Top recalled from other Russians he had met in the past, Bluebeard used a branch he had broken off one of the stunted pines to sweep leaves and dust from the road over the disturbed earth, so as to make it appear that it had never been disturbed. Already they had dumped the two cops' motorbikes over the edge of a ravine. With luck they would never be found, Top told himself, as he wiped the beads of sweat from his brow and walked over to where Jo-Jo was repairing her face with the aid of the Wartburg's mirror.

She had already changed her tights, which had been ripped when she had jumped on the cop's back. Now with the aid of perfume, powder and lipstick, she was beginning to look her usual self again, though the hand which held the lipstick still trembled noticeably.

'How's it going, Jo-Jo?' asked Top, standing a little to one side to admire her. Gee, she really *was* a honey!

'Fine, Top, fine,' she said with a radiant smile that displayed her beautiful white teeth to best advantage.

'Thanks,' he said simply. 'Thanks a lot.'

'Think nothing of it,' she said, licking her lips to moisten them and giving herself one last look of approval in the little fly-specked mirror before straightening up.

Top gazed at her in undisguised admiration for a moment, before lowering his voice and flinging a glance over his shoulder to where Bluebeard laboured, apparently fully absorbed in his task, grunting periodically with the unwonted effort. 'What did you make of him?'

'Yuri?'

'Yeah.'

She frowned abruptly. 'You mean the way he froze back there when the cop jumped you?'

He nodded. 'I mean, Jo-Jo, why didn't he mix it too? It's his life on the line as well as ours – perhaps more so. Langley could have bought us out if the Commie dinks booked us, but not him. No way. So why did he just stand there? He's a well-known scam artist from way back, so why didn't he *do* something?'

Jo-Jo's beautiful face looked thoughtful.

She shrugged. 'Perhaps he couldn't bring himself to kill one of his own people?'

Top shook his head. 'No way, Jo-Jo. From what I know of that jerk's record, he's killed more Russians in that Gulag of theirs* than the whole of the Firm** put together.'

'Yeah, yeah,' she agreed, her voice sombre. 'I guess you're right, Top. It *is* kinda strange. But–'

Suddenly her words were drowned by the shrill shriek of a ship's siren.

They turned as one. The SS *Varna* had begun to move. A faint cream of water had appeared at her elegant bow. She was moving slowly towards the port to pick up her cruise passengers for the voyage home.

Over at the graves, Bluebeard dropped his branch hurriedly. 'We go!' he called excitedly, suddenly recovering his old spirits. '*Davai*! Disneyland, I come!' He wiped his sweating palms on the knees of his trousers and looked from Top to Jo-Jo expectantly.

For one more moment, feeling the comforting hardness of the little silenced pistol in his pocket, Top stared at the Russian defector's fat, glowing face uncertainly, still

* The Soviet concentration camp system
** The CIA

120

wondering about that strange hesitancy with the cops. Then he dismissed the episode from his mind. Behind him the ship's radio system started to blare out in a thick brassy bass: *'Mussi denn ... Mussi denn ... Zur Stadle hinaus'* to welcome the West German tourists back on board after their week on the Black Sea. 'Into the auto, quick!' he ordered. 'Let's get on the goddam stick now... Time's running out!'

Later, much later, Ed Gilmour, alias Top, would realise just how quickly time had begun to run out for him at that particular moment under the burning August sun. But by then there would be nothing that he could do to prevent the inevitable...

BOOK THREE

Mucking about in Boats

'There's something about a sailor, there is something about a sailor, which is fine, fine, fine.'

Old Music Hall Song

1

*'Fill dat barge ... Tote that bale ... Get a lil'
drunk and yo land in jail,'* Corporal
Ramsbottom intoned in a mock version of
Paul Robson. Behind him, Rifleman
Bahadur crooned some ditty in his own
tongue, his brown face gleaming in the heat,
as the Alpha Team, under Lieutenant
Mallory's command, strained at the canal
lock windlass. Slowly the gate began to
creak open to allow their barge, the
Normandie, to glide through to the still,
green water of the canal beyond.

Happily the lock-keeper looked up from
gathering snails from the bushes and waved
to them, and then as an afterthought, gave
them the clenched fist salute.

Mallory grinned. 'He obviously thought
that was the *Volga Boatman's Song*, Ramsbottom,' he said, his face pleasantly flushed
with the heat and the wine they had drunk
with their picnic lunch.

'Bluidy reds, the whole Frog bunch of
'em!' Ross growled, angry as ever. 'And will

yer take a look at the mon, eating yon worms! Disgusting, it is. It's no civilised, I tell yer.' He spat over the side into the water. 'Frogs' legs and worms and yon muck they're allus digging up from the earth with them pigs o' theirs – triffles!'

'Not like *some* people yer could mention, eh Sarge?' Rogers said, and winked at the others, who were stripped to the waist, their lean, muscular bodies bronzed a deep brown. 'That lot what fills sheep's bladders with meat and stuff and eats 'em... Only when they're pissed, of course. Couldn't stand the pong otherwise, I suppose. Haggis, I think they call 'em.'

Sergeant Ross spluttered impotently for a moment before he found his voice. 'Leave off the haggis, yer ignorant sassenach pig! What d'ye ken about good food?'

Mallory smiled again and increased their speed. Now that the *Normandie* was safely through the lock his crew could relax once again. With a weary sigh, Rogers slumped on the deck and took up yet another of the soft porn magazines he had bought immediately they had picked up their barge at the holiday centre on the Canal du Nord. Ross took his position at the prow, eyes to their front as if he half-expected a fleet of enemy ships to appear on this peaceful waterway at any moment; while Ramsbottom settled down once more to the long letter he was writing to his 'lass' back in Pompey. As for the Gurkha, he resumed his ritual sharpening of his beloved *kukri*, his skinny body swaying back and forth as he crooned some obscure *Gurkali* song to himself.

For two days now they had been cruising through the flat French countryside between lines of still poplars and past golden, freshly cropped wheatfields. The landscape seemed strangely deserted. More than once Mallory had told himself that they might well have been the last men alive on the earth. Yet the odd fisherman and lock-keeper glimpsed every now and again, plus the lazy wisps of blue smoke on the horizon, told him that they were not alone. There were, indeed, other people alive in this sun-drenched, lazy countryside. Unlike England, France just happened to be a big country with plenty of open spaces that weren't jam-packed with people.

Twice of an evening, Mallory had allowed his crew ashore to tramp to the nearest hamlet to bring back food and wine, careful to send Corporal Ramsbottom along both times to watch Ross's razor-sharp temper and Rogers' wandering eye with the local girls, while he and Bahadur stayed behind and kept watch. For even in France, he knew from C's instructions that he had to be on his guard. The Communist Party was very strong, particularly along the valley of the Rhône which they would soon be approaching, and they still lived – and acted – in the tradition of the *Maquis*, which during the war had taken the law pretty much into its own hands.

'*You will proceed down the French north-south canal network (see appendix one),*' ran their instructions, couched as always in that cold, bureaucratic Whitehall jargon that was capable of reducing even the most impossible adventure into a dry-as-dust routine. '*Your objective will be the port of Marseilles. Here you will board the cruise-liner the SS Varna, port of origin Odessa (for details see appendix two) and remove Mr Y. Serov, codenamed "Bluebeard" (see appendix three for details of subject and companion(s)). Utmost care will be taken that this mission is not revealed to unauthorised personnel/foreign nationals etc. Escape route is detailed in appendix four.*'

'Well, I'll go to our bloody house!' Ramsbottom had exclaimed when Mallory had revealed the mission to them on their first night out. 'Nicking a Russian from the Yanks! A right old turn-up for the books, sir!'

Ross had wiped the sweat from his crimson, angry face with the back of his hand and flashed a hard look at Mallory. 'Ay, typical, ain't it? Them fancy-pants in London don't know their head fra their arse! Diabolical! Them Yanks of the CIA aren't gonna stand around an' let us nick their tame Russki just like that! So what are we gonna to do, if they start any trouble, I ask ye?' He glared defiantly at Mallory as if he were responsible for the whole business. '*Waste 'em*?'

'No, Ross,' Mallory had answered hastily, knowing Ross's hair-trigger temper. 'This time we really are going to be the tippy-toe boys. In and out, without any trouble. Snatch-and-skedaddle.'

Ross had given him a contemptuous look. 'Ay, some folk'd believe anything,' he had said scornfully.

'Will there be a gong in it?' Robson had asked, as always eager to add another decoration to his collection, so that he could impress the girls back at Poole and Pompey.

'Ay, a putty one!' Ross had sneered.

Only Rifleman Bahadur, his face suddenly very oriental and impassive in the yellow light cast by the hissing gas lantern, had shown no emotion, neither excitement nor anger. Instead he had said in his own tongue solemnly, *'Kafar hune bhanda morne vamro.'*

'Hold yer huish, Gunga Din,' Ross had commanded. 'None of yer heathen blether here.'

Bahadur had remained silent after that, but a sudden chill had run the length of Mallory's spine as he heard the words and he had felt the small hairs at the back of his neck stand eerily erect. He had understood the old Gurkali phrase: 'Better dead than a coward.' What did the little Gurkha mean by it? Could he see things that they couldn't? But Bahadur's dark, bright, unwinking eyes had revealed nothing...

That had been on the first evening. Now Mallory had almost forgotten the little incident as they chugged steadily southwards towards Marseilles. In a way C had been right when he had told them they would be going on a cruise. All he hoped now was that they didn't meet 'all sorts of exciting people' on the way, as C had promised. For Mallory knew what 'exciting people' meant in the Head of Intelligence's

130

book: trouble – plenty of bloody trouble!

Now, as the dragon-flies went skimming lazily over the surface of the water, with here and there a soft *plop* as a trout or some other fish rose for its prey, Mallory briefed his men with the details of the next leg of their slow journey to Marseilles.

'We've about done the Maine-Rhine Canal,' he explained. 'Soon we'll hit the barrages – that's the flow-barriers at Gigny and Port Bernalin on the Seine-Rhône. At the big city of Lyons we'll move onto the River Rhône itself. They say it's a dangerous one to navigate, with fast currents and sandbanks and the like, but I'm sure that that couple of hours we spent back in Poole Harbour will stand us in good stead.'

There were a few lazy laughs from the team. The SBS training school at the little coastal town usually weeded out ninety percent of the volunteers from the Royal Marines for the Special Boat Service, and that included many men who came from 42 Commando. SBS trained sailors and canoeists were among the best in the world. People like Bahadur, for instance – and there were plenty of them in the SBS – were among some of the world's most accomplished fast-water canoeists.

'What about tonight, sir?' Rogers asked hopefully, looking up from a picture of two women with cropped hair doing something unpleasant to each other with a broom handle. 'Can we go ashore?'

'Yes, we'll lie up just beyond Gigny. Corporal Ramsbottom will take a party ashore to buy some food.' He looked solemnly at the grinning young Marine with his spotty face and wistful look in his eyes. 'But no nooky, understand? Just food and wine.'

'Wanker's doom, that's what you'll get, young'un,' Ross threatened, 'if you go on reading yon filthy books. Hair'll grow on the palms of ye hands.' He looked at Mallory. 'Canna we no buy some real grub, sir, tonight?' he asked, an uncharacteristic note of pleading in his tough Gorbals voice.

'What do you mean, *real* grub, Sergeant?'

'Well, none o' them stinkin' cheeses and bits o' potted meat full o' that garlic muck. Perhaps a tin o' bully or two and some piccallili to get it down with – and some proper bread, sir.' Ross's face contorted miserably. 'Yon Frog bread is a pain! Can they no make the real stuff, thick-sliced and in grease-proof paper, like back home?'

Mallory laughed. 'Well, after successfully demolishing the French *haute cuisine*, Ross,

132

I think you deserve your bully and piccallili. Yes, buy what you like, as long as you bring back a decent bottle of plonk, Ramsbottom. Clear?'

'Clear, sir,' Ramsbottom answered dutifully in his solid Yorkshire fashion. He winked at a grinning Mallory. 'And I'll try in my best French to see if I can get a haggis for the sarge here.'

It was beginning to grow dark rapidly, as the little party edged its way along the canal path back to the boat, arms laden with bags from which protruded the long thin French loaves – Sergeant Ross would have to do without his 'thick sliced' this evening. A pale, spectral moon was already beginning its ascent into the velvet summer sky above the poplars, but its light was still shadowy, making the going uncertain. Somewhere to the right, the bull-frogs had begun to croak. Otherwise there was no sound save for the solid plod of their tired feet on the sun-baked towing path. Once more it seemed that the handful of SBS men were alone in the world.

But they knew it wasn't true. A mile behind them lay the hamlet where they had bought food at the little shop, a tumble-down collection of red-brick houses grouped around one of the slate-roofed churches typical of the area. 'Nothing to write home about, Corp, is it?' Robson had commented, as they had wandered across the little square complete with public wash house and the usual statue of Marianne, showing plenty of bronze breast, clutching the *tricoleur*, and protecting a fallen *poilu* of the First World War who had died for *la Patrie*. 'Not what yer'd call swinging exactly.' Eying an old crone with an enormous double goitre, he had cracked, 'Crikey! Look at that old bag. Got her tits right underneath her chin! Do you think they've got their thing in the old place, too?'

'Knock it off,' Ramsbottom had warned. 'Remember the old hearts-and-minds bit. Try to win the natives over.'

But the 'natives' were not to be won over. The woman behind the counter of the little shop, heavy with the smell of garlic sausage and goat cheese, had been unfriendly, and the man at the bar of the *Café de la Paix* had been surly, thrusting their beers towards them over the zinc-covered counter without a word. They had downed it hastily, feeling the eyes of the other patrons fixed on their backs like daggers. It was only after they had left that conversation had broken out again. The three of them, Robson, Ramsbottom and Bahadur, had been glad when they had cleared the place and were on their way back to the barge. More than once, Bahadur, the product of a primitive society which still believed in spirits and ghosts, had flung a glance over his shoulder fearfully and said, 'Frog no good... Think bad things.'

'Yeah,' Robson had agreed, grabbing at his crotch, '*I* think bad things back there, as well, Gunga Din. But it was no bloody good. There wasn't a bird there under the age of sixty!'

Now they were almost back to the *Normandie*, and all three of them were relieved. Stolidly they plodded on to the regular croaking of the bull-frogs and the whirr of the invisible insects skidding across the still green expanse of the canal. Already a thin grey mist was rising now that the heat of the day had abated, and the three men were wading through it up to their knees, seeming to float across the surface of the earth like grey, silent ghosts.

On board the *Normandie*, Mallory looked at his watch for the umpteenth time, as the mist grew steadily thicker, creeping up and curling itself around the anchored barge like a still grey cat.

'Should have been back by now, Sergeant,' he commented.

Ross, who was squatting on the still warm deck next to him, busily cutting his toenails with his clasp knife, looked up. 'Ach, ye ken them three, sir. They'll have stopped off in the local boozer to have a jar. They're na worried about our supper.'

'Suppose you're right.' Mallory shivered a little, for some reason he couldn't quite define. Somewhere an owl had begun to hoot eerily. 'Hope they get their skates on, though. If this mist thickens any more, they could quite well miss us.'

'More than likely, sir,' Ross said calmly, turfing out dirt from beneath a great jagged toenail. 'Yon lot could get lost in Poole Harbour. Lot o' soft nellies.'

In spite of his unreasoning apprehension, Mallory smiled softly. Trust Old Ross. He never let up. He probably wouldn't even smile on his wedding day – assuming there was any female tough and long-suffering enough to want to marry him, which seemed unlikely. 'Why did you ever join the Marines, Ross?' he asked, changing the subject, trying to forget the mist and the eerie quality of the evening.

Ross paused at his task and looked at him, hard and challenging. 'Cos the dustbin lids froze up in Glasgow, sir! In the winter of seventy-four. That's why, sir. Hunger!'

Mallory knew the answer was meant as a challenge. Ross detested his background – that of a wealthy old Etonian who could have taken a token job in the City and never done a stroke of real work in his whole life. As an officer and a man, Mallory knew that Ross respected him; the whole team did. They knew he was capable of doing anything they could do – and more besides. Yet his background was always there, and it always caused resentment. Even Ramsbottom, who had long since out grown his socialist upbringing in the 'People's Republic of South Yorkshire', was not altogether at ease with Mallory at times.

'Tough titty, Ross,' he said softly, playing it cool. 'But if they hadn't frozen up, you wouldn't have been enjoying this pleasure cruise in Central France now, would you, and enjoying the delights of French cuisine...'

Suddenly he stopped off. To the right, in the direction of the village, muted a little by the growing mist, there was the crack of a rifle, sharp, clear, decisive, like the sound a dry twig makes underfoot on a hot summer's day.

Ross dropped his knife onto the deck. He looked hard at Mallory, his face set and intent in the glowing darkness. 'Hunting rifle, sir?' he rasped.

'No way, Ross!' Mallory snapped, springing to his feet. Along the mist-shrouded towpath, someone was running towards the barge – and whoever it was was evidently in a very great hurry. 'Right, down below! Break out the MPs. At the double now!'

'*Sir*!' Ross barked, one hundred percent the professional noncom now. In his bare feet he doubled away to where they had hidden the little German machine pistols in one of the bulkheads.

Mallory tensed, eyes narrowed to slits as he tried to penetrate the billowing white clouds of mist rolling across the canal. The sound of running feet was getting louder. From far off there were cries, too, in French – angry cries, like those of men who had allowed their prey to escape from them.

Suddenly Ramsbottom's familiar bulk burst out of the mist, parcels of food and wine still clutched to his heaving chest. He saw Mallory crouched there tensely at the bow of the barge and gasped, 'Thank God we found you, sir!' He stumbled and almost fell.

Behind him, Rogers and then Bahadur appeared, chests heaving madly, the gleam of the *kukri* in Bahadur's hand.

'What in God's name happened?' Mallory cried in alarm, as Ross came up from below, the little machine pistols in his hands, little red eyes gleaming and ready for a fight. 'Speak up, Corporal! Who fired that shot?'

Ramsbottom skidded to a stop and let his parcels fall at his feet. 'Don't know, sir. All I know is someone fired and we took off. There was a funny lot o' folk back there. I just thought–'

'But how do you know the shot was fired at you, Ramsbottom? *That's* what I'm trying to get at!' Mallory demanded angrily, eyes still trying to penetrate the gloom.

But it was Marine Robson, not Ramsbottom, who answered Mallory's question. With unusual gravity for him, he held up his parcel. *'This* is why, sir.'

Mallory stared. A great jagged hole had been ripped in the paper and one of the wine bottles had been smashed to pieces. Now the dark red wine dripped from the glass débris like blood...

2

'Gives me the creeps,' Robson said in a hushed voice, peering into the white gloom, while next to him aft, Bahadur held his *kukri* at the ready, face set in grim ruthlessness. 'Waiting like this.' He licked his dry lips. 'I mean, if there is anybody out there, why don't they bloody well show themselves and let's get on with it!'

Bahadur remained obstinately silent, gaze fixed on the canal, the only sound his own shallow, controlled breathing, and the insistent nerve-racking croak of the bull-frogs. A long, long way off, a lonely train howled through the night, whistle shrieking like a demented banshee.

Robson jumped. 'Bloody hell, what's that?' he whispered anxiously, edging a little closer to the other man.

'Train,' Bahadur said out of the side of his mouth. 'Hold trap. Talk too much. Can't hear when come to banjo.'

'What the hellus is that supposed–' Robson began, suddenly angered by the Gurkha's

140

strange fractured English. But he broke off abruptly. All of a sudden, the bull-frogs had fallen silent. What did it mean?

Up front with Ross, Mallory also noted the sudden silence and cursed, wishing that he knew more about nature. Did the abrupt ending of the froggy chorus mean trouble?

'Ye ken, sir,' Ross whispered, mouth close to Mallory's ear, 'I'm no so sure that this ain't a false alarm.'

'What do you mean, Ross?'

'Well, sir, why would the Frogs want to banjo us, even if Robson was telling the truth? Ach; that mon could be seeing things. All them porn books and bashing his bishop an' the like!' Ross added scornfully. 'You cannae trust them wankers.'

'Well, he didn't burst that bottle of wine with his penis, Ross,' Mallory snapped severely, his eyes remaining glued to his front. 'Something hit it all right. Who knows,' he shrugged, 'anything's possible these days. Perhaps they know about our mission and are trying to stop us.'

'But who's *they*, sir?' Ross said, voice full of scornful disbelief.

Mallory cursed under his breath. In his stubborn Scottish fashion Ross had hit the nail on the head. Who *were* their attackers, if there were any of them out there? He could hardly visualise the Yanks trying to stop them in this manner. A protest by their embassy in London to the FO would soon have put paid to their mission; that was why C had gone to such great lengths to meet and brief them in that obscure Yorkshire airfield and smuggle them out of the country in secret. 'Communists, I suppose,' he said uncertainly.

Ross laughed softly, his scorn all too obvious. 'Weel, sir, if the Commies know about us and what we're up to, then they'll know about this Bluebeard git as well and make bluidy short work o' the Yanks' attempts to get him out o' Soviet bluidy Russia, won't they, *sir*?' Ross said, with particular emphasis on the last word.

The tough noncom's logic was unassailable, Mallory had to admit. He had reasoned it all out better than many a professor of natural science. If the Russians did know about their mission, then they should know about the Bluebeard caper too and everything was to no purpose. He bit his bottom lip. Perhaps Ross was right. Could it have been a poacher or some poor-sighted hunter who had fired the bullet through Rogers' bottle of plonk? He knew from experience

142

that the French shot anything and everything that might be edible, with or without
a permit. They were the meanest people in
the world, always scavenging for anything
that might save them a sou. Didn't they eat
dandelions as a salad? You couldn't sink
lower than that.

'Well, what do you think, sir?' Ross
persisted. 'Shall I stand the men down? My
guts are doing a back flip-flop, I'm that
starved! I could go some grub now.'

Mallory was just about to concede that the
noncom was right and give out the order to
stand the men down and let them get on
with cooking supper when there was a
splash. Next to him, Ross started and
brought up the little machine pistol in a
flash. 'Did ye heed that, sir?' he hissed.

'Yes. Could have been some river creature,
a duck, perhaps?'

'No way!' Ross snapped. He sniffed suddenly. 'And can ye smell that, sir? Fuel of
some kind.'

'It's oil ... diesel or something,' Mallory
agreed. He gripped his weapon more tightly
in a hand that was suddenly damp with
sweat, and peered desperately into the mist.
'What the hell's going on out there?'

'Sir.' It was Ramsbottom, whose task it was

to patrol the length of the barge between Mallory and Ross and the other two aft.

'What is it?'

'They're out there all right, sir,' Ramsbottom whispered, his broad Yorkshire voice as calm as ever. 'They're rolling some sort of drums along the path. Just caught a glimpse of them back there.'

'Oil drums.' Mallory confirmed what he had seen. 'We thought we just smelled one to our front.'

'What d'yer think they're up to, sir?' Ramsbottom asked in bewilderment.

Mallory had no time to answer. Indeed, he didn't know himself what was going on out there, save that it spelled danger for Alpha Team. Instead, he rapped, 'which way were they going with the barrels?'

'Up front, sir.'

Mallory bit his lip. That was where they had heard the sound of the first barrel being tipped into the water. His mind was made up. 'Ramsbottom.'

'Sir!'

'Slip back to the cockpit and aft. Cut the tether rope. Don't try to get onto the bank to do it. Just slit it.

'Sir!' Ramsbottom answered smartly, in that dogged, no-nonsense manner which made him such a good man in a tight corner.

'Then start up the engine. Soon as I give the command, *back* the barge down the canal. Did you get that? *Back her.*'

'Back her it is, sir,' Ramsbottom replied swiftly. 'That it, sir?'

'That's it. Off you go. At the double now!'

Ramsbottom hurried away.

'Shall I give them a burst over their heads?' Ross snarled. 'Frighten 'em off, sir?'

'No,' Mallory commanded hurriedly. 'We don't want to attract any attention. We want to get through this without using firearms if possible. Besides, we might hit an innocent party.'

'*Innocent!*' Ross was about to protest, but stopped short. There was another splash further up the canal as yet another barrel was tipped into the water.

'Christ,' Mallory cursed angrily. 'What the hell are they up to, whoever *they* bloody well are?'

Suddenly it happened. A soft *plop*. A splutter of angry red sparks streaking through the white mist, and an instant later the river to their front erupted in a flash of bright crimson flame. Mallory reeled back as the grenade exploded and with a great *whoosh*

145

the oil drum rocking violently in the water burst into flame.

'Back off!' he cried frantically, as Bahadur severed the tether rope with one sweep of his deadly *kukri*. Meanwhile yet another oil drum exploded into flame and a scarlet wave, burning away the mist before it, started to advance on the barge.

Mallory saw it in a flash. Accidents happened all the time on board these holiday barges. Amateur sailors were always setting the butane gas stoves alight or over-turning the paraffin heaters. Whoever was attacking them was attempting to fake an accident; yet another tragi-comedy of some weekend sailor setting his craft afire. Hadn't they done a similar thing back in the late seventies with the old German Peiper? They had set his house on fire with a petrol bomb too. It was only later that the medics had found the slugs in his charred, shrunken corpse. Now those shadowy figures out there, rolling ever more oil drums down to the water's edge, were going to do the same to Team Alpha – *if* they could get away with it...

'Start up, Ramsbottom... For Chrissake, Ramsbottom... *Back off*." Mallory shrieked in a paroxysm of fear, as the terrifying wave

146

of fire rushed to embrace the little boat. *'Hurry!'*

Desperately, his eyes bulging out of his crimson face, Ramsbottom pressed the starter button. *Nothing*! He hit it again. Nothing but a low frustrating whine. Behind, Robson cried, 'For fuck's sake, Corp, start the bugger or I'm off over the bleeding side!'

'Naff off' Ramsbottom cried through gritted teeth. His thumb reached out for the damned starter again. Suddenly, for the first time since he had been kicked out of Sunday school for trying to look up the teacher's skirt, he found himself praying.

Now the wave of flame was only yards away. Standing crouched at the bow, Ross and Mallory held their hands before their faces, already feeling the heat begin to suck the very air from their lungs, their faces contorted with fear at the scarlet horror about to consume them. Then, just as the first fiery fingers reached out to clutch the hull, the water hissing and spitting, the paint already beginning to bubble under the tremendous heat, the motor sprang into noisy life!

Mallory felt his legs turn to water. All energy drained out of him and his shoulders sagged as if he had just run a great race. Now they were moving backwards into the mist to their rear, and the flames were vanishing like a horrid nightmare in the moment of awakening. They were safe – for the time being...

'What now, sir?' Robson asked, as the little barge ground to a halt just in front of the lock, which could only be a matter of yards away in the mist.

Mallory wiped the sweat off his face with a hand that smelled of burning – perhaps the heat had singed the small hairs on his arm. 'Well, I somehow suspect they're not going to let us get away that easily,' he said reluctantly.

'What do you mean?' Ross snapped angrily, barely remembering to add a 'sir' to his question. 'Let 'em sodding well come.' He slapped the little machine pistol slung over his shoulder. 'We'll show the bastards.'

'No – they won't make it that easy for us,' Mallory pacified him hastily. 'All right – so they know we've backed off, and they probably know just how far we can go.' He nodded to where the lock would be in the mist. 'If the lock-keeper's smart, he'll probably already have done a bunk.'

'You mean, they're waiting for us to go ashore and open the lock ourselves, sir?' Ramsbottom asked.

'Exactly.'

'I go, sir!' Bahadur piped up. 'Use *kukri*... No mess. Gurkha plenty bottle... Banjo all by self. Gurkha not afraid.'

'I know he isn't, Rifleman Bahadur,' Mallory reassured him. 'But I'm not chancing any of our lives out there on land.'

Bahadur's face dropped and he looked forlornly at the *kukri*, as if he longed to see it run red with human blood.

'Well, what are we going to do, sir?' Ross cried. 'We cannae sit here on our duffs a' night, can we? We've gotta *do* something. Ye ken we're supposed to be yon bluidy professionals they're allus bletherin' about!'

Mallory looked straight at him. 'Sergeant Ross,' he said very quietly and with great dignity. 'We *are* the professionals. Nobody comes more professional than the Special Boat Service, you know that; and Team Alpha is the number one SBS outfit.'

There was a murmur of agreement from the others. Suddenly Ross looked almost ashamed and mumbled a gruff, 'Sorry'.

'We are the élite of the professionals, and the élite don't let themselves get wasted.

149

They waste the other side or duck out smartly before the enemy knows what they're up to. So, we're going to duck.'

'*How*?' his men asked as one.

'Like this. We're going to catch them with their proverbial knickers around their ankles...'

3

The Peeper swallowed hard. For the umpteenth time he pinched himself, hoping to find that this wasn't really happening. That it was a bad dream from which he *must* surely awake at any moment...

'But *Boris*,' he had protested back in London at that gay pub where he had met his Russian contact for the second time, after delivering the photos of that strange meeting at the remote Yorkshire airfield, 'I'm only a photographer, a living camera – nothing more.' Urgently he had grabbed the big Russian's hand. 'A hack ... gay as well... What use could I be to your people over there, Boris?'

But the Russian had been adamant. 'It will be a paid summer holiday,' he had insisted, 'courtesy of the KGB.' And he had flashed the worried photographer a gleaming stainless-steel smile.

Almost before he had been aware of what was happening to him, he was on the Aeroflot flight to Paris (economy class – the

KGB wasn't *that* generous) and hurtling down the *auto-route* to Lyons in a big Citroen packed with hard-faced Frenchmen who scarcely exchanged a word with him for the whole three-hour journey. Next day he found himself being interviewed by the man they called the Count – though for the life of him, he failed to see how a count could wind up in the French CP.

'Sit,' the Count had ordered through ancient lips that were wrinkled like prunes. Then as an afterthought, he had taken his yellow false teeth from the glass on the table in front of him in that big, echoing, musty room and inserted them with a dried-up claw of a hand.

The Peeper had obeyed the command, sitting nervously on the edge of the tall, upright wooden chair, which like everything else in the place seemed a couple of centuries old.

'No doubt you will want to know why we have brought you here?' the Count had said, with hardly a trace of accent. 'I shall tell you. You will identify the men you saw on the airfield for us.'

'But – but you already have the photographs!' he had protested, adding a hasty 'Sir'. The ancient Frenchman, who seemed almost buried in his overstuffed, brocade chair, had an air of authority about him which he felt warranted that form of address.

'Not enough. We want a personal identification before we take action.'

'Take action?' he quavered anxiously.

'Yes,' the old man replied after what had seemed a long time during which the heavy silence of that big room had been broken only by the steady metallic tick of the ornate ormulu clock on the marble mantel-piece. 'They are to be eliminated, after you have identified them. Killed – *by accident.*'

The Peeper's alarm must have been only too evident, for the Count had chuckled throatily and then lapsed into a fit of coughing which had left him flushed a hectic red and spluttering. 'Forgive me ... please,' he had gasped, his yellow, wrinkled features creasing into a smile. 'But old men like to spring surprises on younger men... Women have gone, food has gone,' he had extended his ancient claws in a Gallic gesture of regret. 'Surprise is all they have left.'

'*Surprise* isn't the bleeding word for it!' the Peeper had cursed to himself, as they had led him away for the last leg of his journey to the unknown. By now his stomach had been rumbling madly with fear and he had felt as if he was going to be sick at any moment.

Now here he was in the middle of nowhere, surrounded by hard, desperate men who smelled of animals and cowshit, just like those country Paddies he had known back home in the old days with the IRA. These Frogs were just as contemptuous of him as they had been. More than once he had protested that he had done the job he had been brought here to do: identify the five men in the barge. Couldn't he go before the trouble started? But Claud, their leader − if that *was* his real name − had merely refused with a grunt, cracking the knuckles of his hamlike hands as if to emphasise his words.

Now, as the flames started to die down over the water, the Peeper stared helplessly around at the faces of the men crouched in the bushes near the towpath. All of them were armed, and while he waited for Claud's orders, one of them was sawing away at the nose of a bullet with his knife, cutting a cross into it and turning it into a dum-dum bullet that would disintegrate with horrific results on hitting its victim. The very thought of seeing someone struck by such a terrible device made the Peeper feel sick again. 'Do we go now, Claud?' he asked hastily. 'They've gone, haven't they?'

Claud, his face narrowed to a gleaming red death's head in the dying flames, looked at the quavering little Irishman contemptuously. 'No,' he said slowly in his careful English, cracking those knuckles of his again. 'They cannot go far. I have other men back there. They must come back here. Tonight we must eliminate them. It is our only chance. So,' he grinned at the other man, but his eyes didn't light up; they remained hard and threatening, 'we remain here till they do.'

'Will you try the – er – same thing?' the Peeper persisted miserably, listening to his guts rumbling again and feeling the hot, green, sickening bile ascending his throat and threatening to flood his mouth with vomit at any moment. God in heaven, why did a delicate creature like him have to be tortured like this?

'Yes, those are my orders, Englishman. They are to be eliminated "by accident". So we make them move...' He stopped short. Beyond the mist up the canal, there came the muted sound of firing.

Claud stopped cracking his knuckles and rapped out something in French too quickly for the trembling Peeper to follow. Immediately, half a dozen of the heavy-set men in their faded blue workmen's overalls doubled away to the concealed truck, presumably to bring more drums of oil. He turned to the Peeper again. 'You, Englishman.'

'I'm not an Englishman,' the Peeper began; but the Frenchman wasn't listening.

'Stay here,' he commanded. 'Do not move.' He looked hard at the Peeper crouching there in the bushes, and the latter saw the sudden cruel light in his eyes. 'It is better not to... In the confusion you might get hurt.' With that he was gone to organise the new attack, leaving the Peeper there, trembling with fear at the sudden realisation that was beginning to dawn on him. 'Hurt,' the French pig had said, but he had meant more. He had meant *death*! The Peeper swallowed hard and looked wildly all around him, as if he were seeking aid there in the glowing darkness, but there was none. He was all alone. 'Holy Mother of Mercy,' he gasped, reverting to the appeals of his Dublin youth, 'they're going to kill me ... I know it.... They are... There's going to be no witnesses...' Kneeling there, he clasped his hands together in the classic pose of supplication and stared crazily at the night sky. 'Mother of God, I've never done any harm to nobody. Please ... *please help me*!' And the Peeper began to sob.

Robson ducked instinctively as the shotgun on shore thundered again, stabbing the grey mist with a flash of angry scarlet.

'Soft nelly!' Ross sneered, as Lieutenant Mallory finished wrapping the dripping wet blankets around him, shivering a little with the cold.

'But they was shooting at *me*, Sarge!' Robson protested, and gave Ramsbottom a hand with the hosepipe, while Bahadur poised at the handle of the pump.

'Have ye got cloth ears, mon?' Ross snapped. 'Did ye no hear what the officer said? They dinna want to shoot ye – though by Christ it wouldna be any loss. It's got to look like an accident.'

'Yes, you're right, Ross. They're just trying to panic us into moving forward again. And you can guess what's waiting–' The rest of his words were drowned by the thunder of the shotgun, and a stream of slugs hissed across the canal to their rear.

'They've panicked *me* all right, sir,' Ramsbottom cried. 'I can feel the wet stuff trickling down me inside leg already.'

Mallory grinned. They were damned good

chaps when all was said and done. What other troops could have taken an attack like this, with no opportunity to fight back? 'All right. Are you ready, men?'

There was a murmur of agreement from the others.

'Good, so you know the drill. Keep under cover the best you can. Ross and Robson, if the going gets too sticky, let them have a burst over their heads. Ramsbottom and you, Bahadur, keep spraying the deck with that hose – and don't forget, keep letting me have a drop. My guess is that it's going to get mighty hot in due course.'

'Bahadur do,' the little Gurkha rifleman said eagerly. 'Plenty bottle. No 'fraid heat.'

Mallory took his place at the tiller and started up the engine. 'Thanks, Rifleman Bahadur, but this one I've got to do myself. Right then, here we go!'

As a fresh burst of shotgun pellets zipped across the canal to slam into the bushes on the other side like heavy monsoon rain dropping on a tin roof, Mallory huddled in the soaked blankets, with only his face free, swung the little barge into the centre of the waterway. A moment or two later the *Normandie* had disappeared back into the mist.

On the bank, a tall, dark figure was saying

urgently into his radio, *'Claud, ils sont partis... Allez vite, Claud... Ils sont partis, les sales cons!'*

Now the Peeper could hear the muted *chug-chug* of the barge coming from the white wall of the mist over the canal. Around him, the French tensed over their stinking drums of crude oil, while Claud stood poised with the termite grenade in his hand. As soon as the English appeared, in would go the oil, to form a film right across the canal which Claud would then ignite with a grenade. This time, however, Claud would ensure there was no escape for the five Englishmen. He would ignite the whole shoot in one go; no dribs and drabs this time. There would be no escape for them. They would be trapped and burned to death helplessly out there.

The Peeper licked his suddenly parched lips. He had no feelings for the Englishmen. They were like all the rest of these gung-ho boys, whatever their nationality: Irish, Russian, American, French or English. They were in it for the adventure and the fun; and when the adventure turned into disaster, they should pay the price. They should expect that the butcher's bill would be presented to them sooner or later.

He and his kind, the gays they were always sneering at, these tough young swaggering heroes, didn't indulge in heroics. They wanted love and peace, not hate and war. So they were cowards. Let the bully boys sneer at them. But at least they were survivors. They lived on, come what may.

The Peeper looked around him cautiously. As the noise of the barge grew ever louder, the French were too intent on their tasks to notice him. Should he try? *Should he?* He had little money, spoke barely any French, and hadn't the foggiest idea where he was. But that didn't matter. Let him get to any big town and he'd find a place. Cruise around the bars in the neighbourhood of the main railway station and he'd be sure to strike lucky sooner or later. He'd pick up someone, or someone would pick up him. Then he'd be safe – among his own kind. Yes, he'd do it. He'd run away.

Hardly daring to breathe, the Peeper started to back into the bushes on hands and feet, his heart thumping like a trip-hammer, nerves tingling electrically. What did they used to say in the old days when they'd played as kids on the banks of the Liffey? *Run away and live to fight another day!* That was it. Well, in his case, he told himself, he'd run away and live to *fuck* another day. Chuckling, he disappeared noiselessly into the bushes...

'*Allez-y*!' The harsh command shattered the brooding, heavy silence of the mist-shrouded canal.

To the front of the *Normandie*, there was splash after splash, as the ambushers rolled the heavy drums, one by one, into the water. Immediately, the night air was heavy and cloying with the stench of escaping oil.

'Here we go!' Mallory yelled, knowing that there was no heed for silence now. He opened the throttle wide and the little barge shot forward. To his front, Ramsbottom, stripped to the waist, started pumping all out, while Bahadur directed the jet of canal water on to the barge's deck.

A grenade sailed through the air, trailing angry sparks behind it. Mallory ducked instinctively as it exploded with a sharp, dry *crack*. Glistening steaming white pellets erupted in abrupt fury. *Whoosh*! Almost immediately the oil that was streaming across the canal from the bobbing cans ignited. Mallory staggered under the impact of the immense blast of heat. For an instant he almost lost control of the tiller. A second later the stream of icy water submerged him from head to toe, and the heat died down almost immediately. 'Keep up the good work, Bahadur!' he cried above the crackle and noise of the inferno as he steered the barge straight for it.

Bahadur shouted something unintelligible and swung the stream of water onto the deck once more, as they drew ever closer to the searing, oil-tinged flames. Now Mallory could make out figures on both banks, starkly outlined against the rising flames, and he could see that one or two of them carried rifles. His heart sank. If one of them panicked or lost his nerve now and fired, he would be finished. Once he was hit and let go of the tiller, the rest of Alpha Team wouldn't stand a chance. None of them could take over in time. They would drift helplessly on the canal till the greedy flames submerged them for ever. Mallory ducked, body tensed, ready for that killing slug.

None came. The men on the bank watched impassively and in silence as the narrow little boat, its paintwork already beginning to bubble and splutter like red-hot fat in that heat, headed straight into the fire – and destruction. There seemed no escape for it. In their very inactivity, they appeared to be saying: *you are doomed...*

4

The Peeper opened his mouth and screamed, but no sound came. His voice had vanished with the terror of it all. Standing there at the end of the little path which led out of the bushes, clearly outlined in the blood-red flames from the canal, stood one of the Frenchmen – the one who had made the dum-dum bullets, his brawny arms crossed over his chest and a knowing grin on his swarthy, self-satisfied face, as if he had been expecting the Peeper all along.

'*Oh, la, la!*' he simpered, in the way 'straights' always spoke when they wanted to take a rise out of gays. '*Ma tante ici – seul. Avec moi.*' He pursed his thick, coarse lips and made a kissing sound. '*Viens à moi, mon petit chou...*' And he stretched out his arms, as if he wanted to embrace the petrified little Irishman. '*Allez vite, je suis pressé.*' He grabbed the front of his bulging overalls significantly. '*Allez – j'attends... Mangez!*'

The Peeper recoiled in horror. How often had this happened to him in the past –

usually in some back-alley behind a pub? Nearly always it was some drunken straight, wanting to boast afterwards to his mates, 'Course, I tried it. But that brown cake ain't a patch on birds, lads!' Only this monster of a hetero didn't want to rape him – *he wanted to murder him*!

The Frenchman laughed throatily and crooked a finger at a petrified Peeper, as behind him the crackling of the flames grew ever louder and the bushes began to turn a delicate salmon pink in the reflected glare of the inferno. '*Viens, chérie. Je t'adore.*' He gave a mock sigh, as if he were some lovesick movie star in a B-film. '*Je te veux...*'

The Peeper found his voice at last. As the Frenchman, advanced upon him, face set in a fake smile, arms outstretched to push him away, he pleaded. '*Don't... Don't! Let me go... Don't you dare touch me, or I'll–*'

The rest of his words were drowned, as the Frenchman's brawny arms enveloped him and he felt himself pressed hard against his overalls, his nostrils assailed by the stink of stale male sweat.

Desperately, sick with fear, already feeling himself beginning to evacuate his bowels with fright, he tried to struggle. But the Frenchman held him effortlessly, as if he were a child, chuckling crazily all the time. He attempted to kick him. The Frenchman swung him off his feet and pressed him even tighter to his big chest, stifling his terrified shrieks. '*Soyez calme, chérie,*' he whispered in a husky, supposedly sexy voice. '*Je suis ton ami.*' He gave a loud sucking noise as if he were planting a great kiss on someone's lips and laughed uproariously, as if it were the greatest joke in the world. Then, gripping the struggling man more firmly in his arms, he turned and started to brush his way through the undergrowth towards the burning canal.

Suddenly, as the terrible heat began to sear his back and his wild eyes took in the sight of the Frenchman's face turning a bright, glowing crimson, the Peeper realised what he was going to do. '*No!*' he screamed, fear making him lose all control. '*No! Not that! Don't...*'

Now the heat on his back was unbearable. He could smell something singeing. Behind him the flames roared. Desperately, his face contorted by overwhelming fear, the Peeper clung to his captive, screaming incoherently, great tears running down his ashen cheeks.

Suddenly the Frenchman grunted. The Peeper could feel his biceps harden. The heat was overpowering now. *'No!'* he shrieked. To no avail. The Frenchman heaved, and the Peeper felt himself hurtling through the air towards the burning water...

The heat was unbelievable. Everywhere the greedy flames leapt up to consume them. The paintwork bubbled and burst, covering the bow of the *Normandie* with a leprous rash of bursting scabs like the symptoms of some loathsome skin disease. Again the jet of water submerged Mallory, as he held onto the tiller grimly. He gasped with relief, feeling himself able to breathe once more.

Huddled in his soaked blankets, which began to steam again as soon as the jet of water had passed, Mallory peered forward. The flames seemed impenetrable. Could they make it through the flaming gauntlet before the *Normandie* began to burn? If they couldn't, none of them would survive in that burning chaos. He shook his head as the heat struck him in the face an almost physical blow, gasping for breath as the heat scorched his lungs. Behind, Ramsbottom and Bahadur saw him stagger, the steam shrouding his tall, bent frame. Immediately they switched the hose round, with Ramsbottom pumping furiously, the sweat pouring down his naked upper body in rivulets.

Now they were in the very midst of the inferno. All was noise, confusion, smoke and the terrifying crackle of the greedy flames. The bow of the *Normandie* began to smoke once more. Already angry blue flames were beginning to appear in the caulking between the wooden planks. Bahadur grunted and swung the hose from a soaked Mallory, sweeping the jet of cold canal water across the deck. The flames retreated, hissing and spitting like live things, angry at being cheated of their victim. The *Normandie* chugged on.

Below, Ross, also naked to the waist and running wet with sweat, peered through the porthole at the billowing flames. His face was tinged black with oil smoke, his finger clutching the trigger of the little machine pistol. Inside, his rage was as fierce and as hot as the flames outside. He felt so impotent. If only he could fire back, let off a burst, kill a few of the treacherous Frog bastards!

Next to him, young Robson, his face looking as if it had been greased with Vaseline, his eyes wild, wide and staring, gasped, 'Sarge, do you think we're gonna make it? I've allus been shit-scared o'fire!'

'Of course we'll make it!' Ross snorted. 'Yon officer and gent up there'll see to that! He'll no let us–' He stopped short, and for once his tough, craggy face revealed fear – absolute, overwhelming, unreasoning fear. 'What in God's name is that?' he quavered, pointing a finger that trembled visibly at the porthole. 'Oh, my God!'

Robson followed the direction of his gaze and gasped too. There was something bobbing up and down in the sea of orange flame outside. It couldn't be described as human. Instead of a face the thing had a black crusted mask. Where the eyes should have been, there were two vivid, suppurating pools. With agonising slowness, the thing raised one charred hand from which the flesh dripped in black folds, revealing a bone which gleamed like polished ivory. For a moment or two the thing's mouth opened to utter meaningless phrases; then it was gone. Robson couldn't help himself. His shoulders heaving violently, he retched, the vomit trickling down his pimply chin unheeded.

Now Mallory sensed they were almost through. The heat seemed less intense, although the forrard deck was smoking heavily once more, and again the little blue flames were beginning to eat up the caulking. Luckily that blessed jet of water hit him again, and for a moment or two that tremendous, all-consuming heat died down. Crouched like a monk under his cowl of soaking blankets, he peered ahead, gasping for breath. Was it possible? Was that *really* a gap in the flames? He jerked the tiller hard. The battered, smoking barge answered immediately. Vaguely, above the roar of the flames, he heard angry cries from the bank to his right. He ignored them. His gaze was set exclusively on that gap. He must reach it. He *must*! Another burst of flame came racing towards the *Normandie* like the searing thrust of a blowtorch. Below, Ramsbottom and Bahadur reacted immediately. Mallory gasped painfully for air as the blast of canal water hit him. Spluttering and choking, he felt the heat waft over him, setting his blankets off steaming furiously again. And then suddenly, blessedly, they were through, and at five knots an hour, they were chugging through flame-free water, leaving that killing inferno behind them.

Exhausted, the men slumped over the pump, Mallory hanging onto the tiller on legs that felt as if they were made of rubber.

Time seemed to pass leadenly. Behind them the crackle of the flames and the angry cries died away. Still the men of Alpha Team didn't move. Slowly, insidiously, the grey mist started to surround the little craft once more, submerging them in its clammy embrace. It was then that Mallory saw it: a sightless charred horror tottering towards him, strange, inhuman sounds coming from its red hole of a mouth, one withering claw held in front of it like the skeletal branch of a winter tree. And he screamed!

The thing which had once been a man died agonisingly at their feet, the charred frame visibly contracting under their awed gaze as the sinews dried out, dragging the wretched creature's limbs into grotesquely contorted positions. It gave off a nauseating stink that had Rogers clutching his throat and Bahadur praying and swallowing fervently at the same time.

Only Ross seemed to be in possession of himself. Kneeling down next to the horror, he patted the still smoking rags for papers and documents, pausing every now and again and daring to bring his head close to that sightless charred monstrosity in an attempt to catch the mumble that came from the scorched lips.

The inevitable happened. Suddenly the monster stiffened, back as taut as a bowstring, claws raised, as if fighting off death, strange bubbling sounds coming from deep down within it.

Mallory recoiled in horror. Bahadur started to chant a prayer in his own tongue. Robson choked and swallowed hard. Only Ross remained unperturbed. 'What d'ye say?' he cried urgently, 'what, mon?' He dared to bend his head even closer to the horror. 'Ay, ay,' he said, 'I hear ye.'

Then it was all over. The thing gave a great eerie moan like the sound a bagpipe makes when deflated. The last desperate strength went from it. It collapsed back on the scorched deck and lay there like a black, petrified log. Slowly, very slowly, Ramsbottom walked across with one of the soaked blankets and draped it across the horrible apparition.

It was a long time before anyone spoke. Now there was no sound save the steady *chug-chug* of the engine and the lapping of the water. Somewhere a long way off, the sound muted by the thick, wet mist, a night creature hooted.

'Well?' Mallory said finally, his voice seeming to come from far away. 'What did you find out, Ross?'

Even Ross seemed subdued by the mood of that moment and the events of this terrible night. His voice was uncharacteristically soft, and for once the anger had vanished from it. 'No much, sir,' he answered softly, even sombrely. 'He was a Mick by his accent, I'd say.'

Robson looked at Ramsbottom significantly, as if the discovery was of importance.

'And I think the Russkis sent him here.' He held up the charred flight ticket. 'From yon Russki airline. Aeroflot.'

'Anything else, Sarge?' Robson asked, in control of his nausea now.

'Nothing,' Ross replied very slowly, as if it were taking a great effort on his part to make his brain function. 'Apart from this.' He held up the charred piece of glossy paper in a hand that trembled slightly.

Hurriedly Mallory flicked on his torch and they crowded forward to see what Ross held in his hand.

For a moment or two they were puzzled. There was only a fragment of the photo left. Then Ramsbottom blurted out, *'Christ, that's Gunga Din here!'*

Bahadur swallowed hard and nodded his

172

head in agreement, as if he was too overwhelmed to speak.

'And that's me!' Robson said in awe. 'I've got me best T-shirt on. You know – me trendy threads.'

'Yes,' Mallory agreed solemnly, 'the one with *Frogmen Do It Underwater* on it.' He hesitated just for a fraction of a second, before saying in a low, depressed voice, 'And you know where you last wore that, don't you, Marine Rogers?'

Rogers thought hard. Suddenly he shot the others a look of alarm. 'Of course! At that bleeding airfield with the SAS – back in Yorkshire!' He flashed a glance from one grim face to the other, hollowed out and hard in the cold white light of the torch. 'But what does it mean, mates?'

'It means,' Ramsbottom said slowly, 'that they've been on to us right from the bleeding start.'

'Ay,' Ross said with a flash of his old anger. 'We've been bluidy well rumbled. They're on to us. They ken what our bluidy mission is!' He dropped the charred photograph unfeelingly on the body crumpled at his feet.

For a moment no one spoke as they all absorbed that chilling piece of information, each man wrapped up in a cocoon of his thoughts, as he began to realise the full implications of this startling intelligence.

'But who are they, sir?' Robson broke the heavy brooding silence at last. *'Who?'* He looked appealingly at the tall young officer.

Wearily Mallory shook his head. 'I don't know, Robson, I really don't. We have an Irish connection... We have a Communist connection, that's for sure. We know we've been observed, perhaps even followed, ever since that meeting on the airfield.'

Robson shivered and flung a glance over his shoulder into the mist, as if he half-expected to find someone out there looking back at him.

'But what their purpose is exactly, we don't know,' Mallory concluded.

'But one bluidy thing we do ken,' Ross snapped. *'Yon buggers, whoever they are, are out to kill us...*

BOOK FOUR

Voyage to the Unknown

'He, the trained spy, had walked into the trap
For a bogus guide, seduced with the old tricks.'

W.H. Auden

1

Top had first met 'Ma' Barker the day the US Army had been run out of Nam. Saigon had been chaos. The missiles had been hitting Tan Son Nhut airport regularly every minute or so as the choppers came clattering in to evacuate the frantic US civilians to the ships waiting offshore. The *Midway* had been right in the centre of it all, the flight deck of the giant aircraft-carrier so packed with choppers that in the end they had been forced to push a half dozen of them – twelve million bucks' worth in all – over the side to make room for fresh ones to land. It was panic at sea and panic on the shore. Refugee women were going into labour on all sides, wounded clogged the gutters, and in the sheds marines were screwing society women, frantic to be taken off before the Cong appeared. Others were too busy raking in fortunes in gold and jewels, to find time for screwing. And into this mess had flown 'Ma' Barker and her 'boys'.

Up on the roof of the Embassy, armed with a shotgun and strung with grenades, Top had been trying to get the shit-scared feather merchants of the State Department off without too much hysteria, when the chopper carrying 'her' – or was it 'him'? – had landed on the flat expanse of baking concrete. Top had done a double-take. There before him was a long, angular beast with no tits he could detect, dropping to the deck, all wrinkled stockings and silver wig, with rocket-launcher gripped in one hand and purse in the other. He had nearly flipped on the spot, as the sweating, harassed marines and what was left of his Green Berets had begun to hoot and laugh. 'Jesus!' he had gasped. 'It's just plain bananas, the whole fucking gizmo – *bananas*!'

'Just curb your tongue, young man!' the tall, angular beast had chided him. 'You are, after all, in the presence of a lady.' Next instant she had blasted off the rocket launcher and a rocket had gone zipping across the capital's roofs into a building which he had long suspected to be a Cong spotter site.

All through that terrible and chaotic day, 'Ma' Barker and her 'boys' had been here,

178

there and everywhere, her 'young men' from State quiet, efficient and somehow very demure, unlike the cursing and harassed, red-faced marines and his own Green Berets, snapping off shot after shot, making the Cong pay for every yard of ground. Afterwards, when they had finally been taken off back to the *Midway*, leaving chaos and shame behind them, and Top and his boys had been calling out 'Gimme a goddam ice-cold beer, willya?' and 'Boy, am I bushed! Where's the fucking rack to get some shut-eye?', 'Ma' Barker had announced demurely, 'I think I'll go to the Ladies' room, if there is such a thing aboard, and freshen up. I'm having dinner with the admiral at seven.' And off she had gone primly, with only the slightest camp sway of her skinny hips, one stocking around her ankle, her silver wig tilted to one side to reveal a completely bald head...

Top had met 'Ma' half a dozen times after that. Wherever the situation got hot, 'Ma' Barker and her 'boys' would surely be there. The boys changed superficially, but in essence they were always the same: polite, well-spoken young men with Ivy League ties and that significant bulge beneath their left armpit, who eyed their boss with a certain reserved awe. A couple of times of an evening in those remote jungle camps of Central America where Americans had fought and died in secret for the last three or four years, Top had heard weird little schoolgirl giggles coming from the direction of 'Ma' Barker's tent. Once he had even caught 'Ma' herself wandering around drunkenly in the night looking for the latrine, clad only in her underwear; and in spite of her well-filled bra, below the plimsoll line she hadn't looked very feminine to his startled gaze. Hastily Top had averted his eyes, only slightly reassured by the fact that 'Ma' Barker had entered the wooden shack reserved for female guerrillas.

Now here she was again, accompanied by four new 'boys' in their well-pressed seersucker suits and Harvard ties, mincing her way up the gangplank at Istanbul. Her wig was golden now, but her long, lanky figure still looked as strange and as unfeminine as ever. Waving to all and sundry, she cast him a significant look as she passed him on her way to her cabin, her dark eyes spelling trouble – lots of trouble.

They met over drinks: good ole American Bourbon on the rocks for Top and lemon tea for Ma, as they sat in the most secluded corner of the passenger lounge.

'This harsh sun simply plays havoc with my skin,' Ma had simpered in the presence of the Russian steward, then waited until he had served and gone before saying, 'Top, there are problems.'

Top took a large gulp of Bourbon. If 'Ma' Barker and her 'boys' were on board the SS *Varna*, he knew that his fond hopes of a little cruise, with plenty of sleep and plenty of booze, were over. She tolerated no slackness; she was like somebody's goddam maiden aunt, of the old school. 'Where's the fire, Ma?' he asked, trying to play it cool.

'Top, so far it's just being kindled, but if it ignites, there could be international complications,' she answered prissily, drinking her tea with her little finger extended so very politely. 'G-2 Army Intelligence in London, in the shape of the Assistant Military Attaché at our embassy there, reports that the British are on to us.' Ma Barker lowered her voice even more as Bluebeard and Jo-Jo entered the lounge and the fat Russian ordered champagne in an outrageous English accent, clapping his fat paws at the stewards as if he were John D. Rockefeller himself.

'The Limeys!' Top gasped. 'What in Sam Hill have they got to do with this caper?'

Ma looked at him primly across the tea-cup and tut-tutted severely. At that distance Top could see the five o'clock shadow around Ma's lean jowls all too clearly. It turned his stomach slightly. 'Please watch your tongue, Top. I know you're used to the rough ways of soldiers and such like, but now you're talking to a delicately brought-up lady. Please, I beg you, remember that.'

'Yes ma'am,' Top said with a gulp.

Opposite him, Ma hitched up her slightly sagging bosom with a jerk of the elbow.

Near the entrance to the lounge the stewards were serving the champagne – a double magnum, at the expense of the American tax-payer, Top noted angrily and Bluebeard was insisting on being allowed to remove Jo-Jo's slipper so that he could drink the sparkling wine out of it.

'How common!' Ma snapped icily. 'One wonders if he's really worth all the fuss we're making over him. He's definitely *not* the type of person I would care to invite into my home.'

'No, ma'am,' Top said dutifully, telling himself that Bluebeard wasn't exactly the kind of guy who would want to be invited; his sexual interests were all too obvious, and they didn't include figures like 'Ma' Barker with her inflated brassière, courtesy Fredericks of Hollywood – no, sir!

Ma forgot the loud-mouthed Russian and resumed her briefing. 'The word is that a group of British covert agents have been sent from the United Kingdom – we don't know how and in what particular direction, but we do know they're on their way – and it's pretty obvious that they're going to make an attempt to take that gross creature from us.' Delicately, with her skinny wrist held at an elegant angle as befits of a lady of breeding, Ma raised the cup to her lips.

Top whistled softly and absorbed Ma's words for a moment. 'Our next port of call is Alexandria,' he said.

'No.' Ma shook the wig, scattering lacquer like golden rain. 'They'd never get into Egypt. Alexandria is out.'

'After that there's Marseilles and an afternoon stopover at the Bay of Rosas, Northern Spain,' he added. 'That's where we lift him off. Bluebeard, I mean.'

Ma considered his words, rubbing her long, red-lacquered fingers across her lean jaw, not seeming to notice the rasping sound of the five o'clock shadow. Finally she spoke. 'Could be it, Top. The French, as you know from Saigon, are a decadent people, given to dreadful perversions that a sheltered woman of my type dare not even think about.' Ma fluttered the long false eyelashes coyly. 'They are easily bribed and as you perhaps know, Marseilles is full of dreadful gangsters – Italian, French, Algerian and the like. Anything's possible there!' Ma sucked her gums thoughtfully, revealing long yellow fangs, while Top stared at her, mesmerised, waiting for her next reaction; for she represented State and State had the final word in this operation, even if he was running the caper for the CIA.

'Of course,' she said, 'we must avoid any wet business with the British unless it's absolutely necessary. It would take a lot of explaining by State if it ever came out. And the British are touchy at the best of times.

'Load of cream-puffs!' Top snorted scornfully. 'Half of them are fruits...' He stopped suddenly and flushed red. 'Sorry ma'am,' he stuttered hastily.

Ma Barker looked at him blandly. 'I don't know why you should be apologising to me, Top,' she announced, and Top blushed even more. Now he was totally confused. What the hell was a guy who dressed up in dame's clothes anyway? A fruit, a fag, a drag queen, or what? He shook his head like a boxer who had just taken a count of nine and was trying to snap out of it before it was too late.

'So,' Ma said, very businesslike now. 'Once we reach Marseilles, we go into a state of red alert, just in case the British try to snatch him at the port. Next problem: what about the opposition on board ship? After all, it's a Russian vessel and the KGB makes quite sure that none of the crew defects during cruises of this nature.' Ma's face hardened and for a moment her voice lost that simpering, fake female falsetto and became very definitely masculine. 'Well, Top, who's the KGB's agent-in-residence? Who's their gun?'

Top shrugged a little helplessly and stared around the big, half-empty lounge to where Bluebeard was on his knees, red-faced with effort and surrounded by laughing stewards as he slopped champagne into Jo-Jo's slipper. 'Gee, I just don't know, Ma... Why,' he concluded with a gulp, 'it could be any one of the goddam Russki jerk-offs... Just *any* one of them.'

For once Ma Barker didn't object to the profanity. Instead she, too, stared around the big, sunlit lounge, gazing at the reflection of the waves in the Bosphorus dancing noiselessly on the walls below the melodramatic portrait of Lenin addressing the revolutionary workers back in 1918. 'I don't know, Top,' she said slowly, 'I really don't know....'

'Know what, Ma?' he echoed, puzzled.

Her strange face took on a worried frown. 'You and I have been on these capers often enough before, Top.'

He nodded his agreement. 'Sure, Ma, that we have.'

'But have you known anything to go as smoothly as this one, Top? Here, you are, with that young lady Miss Johns – talking of which, I wonder if she should show that much thigh in front of the stewards? The Russians aren't used to seeing so much female flesh displayed in public. No matter. Where was I?'

Top drew his eyes reluctantly from where Jo-Jo half-lay on the overstuffed couch, her skirt thrown back to reveal a plump white thigh above sheer black silk stockings. 'You were saying something about it being easy – this caper.'

'Yes. That's it! Somehow, Top, it's too easy, much too easy.' Abruptly Ma Barker was all man, her voice harsh and demanding. 'D'ya know, Top, I think the whole goddam thing *stinks*!'

2

'They're tailing us, sir … I'm certain,' said Ramsbottom, from a crouched position in the back of the hired Renault. 'I've been watching that dark blue Citroen for the last fifteen minutes, and everywhere we go, like Mary's lamb, they seem to go as well.'

'Ach, the heat's getting at yer brain, mon!' Ross snarled, and turning with difficulty in the cramped, hot car, twisted round to stare to their rear along the dusty, blinding-white country road. 'Who'd want to follow us?'

They had abandoned the battered barge just before they had reached Vienne on the Rhône, taken an early morning bus full of Algerian factory workers into town, hired the Renault for two days and, leaving the main *route nationale* and heading south to the next city on the way to Marseilles, Valence, had pushed into the foothills leading to the Alps.

Mallory had known when he had made his somewhat amateurish attempt at evasion that they stood a chance of being picked up again by whoever had attacked them on the canal. After all, there was no mistaking them for anything but soldiers, and their French was limited. Nonetheless he had hoped that they might have escaped being spotted again until they could disappear into the seething rabbit-warren of Marseilles. They were still quite a way off the main route to the south.

'Are you sure, Corporal?' he asked over his shoulder, crouching next to Robson, who was driving.

'Can't be sure, sir, of course,' Rams-bottom replied dutifully. 'But the other driver's making no attempt to overtake us. The road's dead straight – no on-coming traffic – and we seem to be about the only people in the whole country who are actually sticking to the ninety-kilometre speed limit for country roads.'

The summer sun was at its zenith. It blazed in a golden ball from the bright blue afternoon sky. Above the spiked outlines of the firs marching up and down the hills on both sides of the road, the heat-haze rippled in trembling powder-blue waves. All seemed so remote, so rustic, so peaceful! Yet there was something somehow sinister and menacing about the black bug-like shape of the big Citroen following them, its wind-screen tinted blue so that it was impossible to see inside it. For all the world it could have been a ghost car, with no one at the wheel.

Mallory licked his parched lips. He would have dearly loved an ice-cold beer. None of them had drunk a drop since early morning, and he hadn't wanted to stop to buy something to quench their thirst until they were well away from the spot where they had abandoned the barge on the Rhône. 'All right, Robson. Bugger the traffic laws. Hit the gas – and let's hope they're not cops!'

'*Sir*!' Robson answered eagerly. He needed no urging. Like most young men he delighted in driving too fast, especially when it wasn't his own car. He pressed down on the accelerator. In spite of its load, the little hired Renault shot forward, and almost instantly a cooler breeze wafted through the car.

Behind them, the other car picked up speed too. Mallory could see it in the fly-specked, dirty rear-view mirror. Now both cars were doing well over 120 kilometres an hour on the narrow country road with the deep drainage ditches on both sides, and Robson, his spotty face gleaming, eyes sparkling, was hunched over the wheel like a professional racing driver.

Mallory timed the spurt forward exactly. One minute... Two... Three minutes... Four... Five minutes, before he commanded above the roar of the overworked engine, 'All right, Nikki Lauda, bring her down to eighty again and we'll see what the Citroen does now!'

A little reluctantly, Robson eased his foot off the accelerator just as the Renault started to tackle yet another incline. The car started to lose speed immediately. Mallory flung a glance at the mirror. The Citroen was doing the same. It was obvious; its driver, whoever he was, was making no attempt to overtake them.

In the back, Ross seemed to read his thoughts. 'Yon frog has nae attention of trying to get by us. Ramsbottom here was right. They're tailin' us, I hae no doubt.'

'What we gonna do, sir?' Robson asked, eyes glued on the road ahead.

Mallory thought for a moment. Then he made his decision. 'All right, chaps, we've got to find out one way or the other.'

'Ay,' Ross agreed. 'It's either piss or get off'n the pot!'

'Exactly,' Mallory said. 'We've got to

check them out. We can't go on playing games for ever.' He turned to Robson. 'The next turn-off right up into the hills, we take it. Clear?'

'Clear, sir!'

'And what then, sir?' Ramsbottom asked.

'As soon as we find a suitable position – *if* they're still following us – we jump them. There's no other way.'

'*Sir*!' Robson cut in, excited now by the thrill of the chase. For him, it was like the movies. He was particularly fond of films involving car chases, especially if preceded by some Californian cracker taking off her threads slowly and seductively.

'What?' Mallory rapped.

'There, sir! Road to the right!' Mallory flung a glance forward. Up ahead was a clump of naked boulders, shimmering in the heat, next to a fading blue and white metal sign indicating a third-class road.

'Take it!' Mallory commanded. 'All right, chaps, get ready to bale out at the double when I give the order. Then–'

The rest of his words were drowned by a howl of protest from the engine, as Robson flung the vehicle from fourth to second gear madly and hit the brakes at the same time. The Renault hissed round the sharp bend on two wheels, the tyres screeching, each rivet in the car seemingly about to burst loose at any moment. Behind them, the country road disappeared in a cloud of blinding white dust.

Robson thrust home third and hit the gas pedal again, and the car rocketed forward, with Bahadur clutching his stomach, his face a shade of green, moaning, '*Oh, oh*! *Feel pukey*! *Lot o' pukey*!' Next moment they were rattling on up the bumpy track, shielded on both sides by boulders and stunted pines.

Next to Mallory, Robson snatched the gear from third to second and careened around a hairpin bend. Mallory, hanging on for dear life, peered ahead. The road was clear. 'What's it look like back there, Ross?' he yelled above the roar.

'So far, so good, sir,' Ross yelled back. 'Nary a sight o' the Frog bastards.'

Mallory breathed out carefully. Perhaps they had been imagining things after all. 'Take it easy now, Robson,' he ordered. 'Let's see if they really are following us.'

'Yes, sir,' Robson replied dutifully, though he would have dearly loved to tackle the curves at speed. He slowed down, while in the back the others peered through the wake of white dust.

'Well?' Mallory demanded.

'Still no sign of them, sir.'

'All right. This is what we're going to do. Next time you come to a bend where you can get off the road, Robson, off you go. Bale out immediately and let's have a real check. Got it?'

'Got it, sir!' they sang out.

A minute later, Robson spotted it – an area of parched yellow grass to the left of the winding, steep road, hidden from behind by several large boulders. He hit the brakes and they went bumping and rumbling off the dusty road right onto the grass, Robson twisting the wheel from left to right frantically in order to avoid the potholes.

'*Out!*' Mallory cried, almost before they had come to a halt, and opening the door, flung himself outside. He hit the grass hard, but next moment he was on his feet and pelting from the boulders which fringed the road, followed by the others, their little machine pistols concealed but ready underneath their jackets just in case.

But there was no need of the weapons. Crouched there, hearts beating furiously, they waited in vain. As the dust finally cleared, it revealed that the little road was empty of life, save for the lizards scuffling back and forth on mysterious errands of their own in the baking summer sunshine. The Citroen hadn't followed up the turn-off. It had gone straight on!

Mallory wiped the sweat from his brow and gave a sigh of relief. The men's nerves were taught as bowstrings after the business on the canal and that charred monster with the sightless eyes. They were seeing attackers where there were none. 'All right,' he said, rising and brushing the dust from his knees. 'Let's take five over there in the shade. We can do with it. I'll have a look-see where we are on the map.'

'Can we eat, sir?' Ramsbottom asked eagerly.

'Of course, if you've still got anything to eat.'

Bahadur groaned once more and hurried over to the nearest drainage ditch.

Robson also groaned. 'Could do with a bit of a break, sir. All this travel does broaden the mind, don't it?' And he rubbed his sore backside.

There were murmurs of agreement from the others all save Ross. As they walked slowly back to the car, he grumbled in his usual surly fashion, 'I hae ma doubts, sir, that I do.'

Ten minutes later they were on their way again. According to the Michelin map, the track they were following would connect with a D-road that would in due course take them down to the valley and back to their original road. Now they climbed steadily, Robson taking it easy with the narrow winding track, while the others, rested from the break, chatted idly, Bahadur, his travel sickness apparently overcome at last, singing tunelessly to himself of his remote Nepalese home.

'Should be coming up to the crossroads soon, Robson,' Mallory directed, following their route on the map spread across his knees. 'As soon as you do, take D352 to the right. It's a bit winding according to the map, but it should bring us down out of the hills just before Montelimar, if I'm not mistaken.'

'Where the nougat comes from?' Robson said with a cheeky grin.

'Where the nougat comes from,' Mallory agreed. 'Fancy a place whose only claim to fame is that they make a sticky piece of candy there.'

Behind them, Ramsbottom was saying to a bored Ross and Bahadur, 'When this little lot is over and Mr Mallory gives us some time off, I'm gonna buy our lass some of that fancy French scent – yon Miss Door stuff. It turns women on, yer know – especially after they've had a bairn or two and get a bit slack between the sheets. Makes 'em right romantic, like, and randy.'

Subject Normal: Sex, Mallory told himself with a lazy grin. All was well with Alpha Team again. The flap had passed. 'All right, Robson,' he commanded, 'take it easy now. We should be–' Suddenly the words froze on his lips. Next to him, Robson acted instinctively. He hit the brakes hard. The Renault shimmied from side to side, carried forward as if on a sliding sledge. Straight ahead of them, a great old oak completely blocked the road, its ancient branches rearing into the sky, almost blotting out the yellow ball of the afternoon sun, so that it seemed that they were skidding straight into a dark green forest.

'For Chrissake!' Ross bellowed, red-faced.

In front, Mallory flung up his hands to protect his face. Then in the very last moment, just when it seemed that nothing could save the car from slamming into the fallen tree, the Renault howled to a stop, filling the air suddenly with the stink of burning rubber and oil.

Robson collapsed face-forward over the wheel with a shocked gasp. Ross cursed. 'What kind o' bluidy country is this! Bluidy trees blocking the sodding roads and nary a sign to warn a feller! Now what can a bloke say to that, eh?'

'What indeed?' Mallory said slowly, as his eyes began to register the fact that the great oak had been deliberately felled to block the road. With a familiar sinking sensation in the pit of his stomach, his gaze fell on the empty packets that had contained the plastic explosive, all too evident in the ditch beyond, and he realised they had walked straight into a damned trap. Like the rankest of amateurs, they had been conned the whole lousy way. Now they were going to get the stick!

3

All was silent. There was no sound, save the steady throb of the engine and the noise of the insects chirping madly in the dusty trees. For what seemed an age, the five of them slumped there in the hot little car, staring at the felled tree. Slowly Mallory stared about him at the stunted scrub and the naked rock, heavy with the scent of pine resin.

'*Crack!*' The snap of a rifle made him jump.

Abruptly a long line of holes stitched the dust alarmingly, accompanied by the mad mechanical chatter of a machine pistol.

'They shoot!' Bahadur cried. 'From rocks!'

As one they swung round. To the left, thin whiffs of grey smoke were drifting from the boulders.

Madly Ross wound down the window at his side, the little machine pistol clasped firmly in his free hand.

'Don't fire back!' Mallory cried, and

knocked the weapon up, just as Ross was about to squeeze the trigger. 'Robson! Down that track to the right!' he ordered desperately, as their unseen attacker fired again and the dirt erupted right across the road in angry little spurts of grey and red.

'Oh, my Christ, sir!' Robson exclaimed in dismay. 'Down *there*, sir?'

'Down there. Come on. Get your skates on!'

Robson took another look at the narrow bumpy track, bounded on one side by naked rock and on the other by a sheer drop to the green valley below, gulped, and thrust home first gear. Just as the line of slugs raced directly towards the car, he let out the clutch and they shot forward, skidding madly round the bend in a whirl of angry white dust and right onto the track itself, the men at the back bouncing up and down crazily as if they were on a trampoline.

Now they were roaring down the track, the echo of their engine deafening in those narrow confines. Robson sat crouched behind the wheel, face streaming with sweat, as if he were driving in the Grand Prix itself, while the valley flashed by at a dizzying rate. In the back, Bahadur, his face green, once more retched miserably into his handkerchief.

'It was a set-up all right!' Mallory yelled above the noise. 'That tree didn't come down of its own accord. It was knocked down. And that sniper didn't just happen to be there!'

'But if that's so, sir,' Ramsbottom protested, urgency in his voice for once, 'why didn't the bugger waste us back there, like? He could have done easy.'

'Remember: whoever they are, they want whatever happens to us to look like an accident, not murder. It was the same back on the canal.'

'I dinna gie a damn about accidents,' Ross snorted angrily, nursing the unused weapon on his lap. 'I'd murder the gits, that I would, no matter!'

'So, sir,' Ramsbottom persisted, 'if they want it to look like an accident, how they gonna do it *now*, sir?'

'Ach, mon,' Ross sneered, 'd'ye think yon officer's bluidy clairvoyant? How should he know?'

'Let's concentrate on getting back to the main drag!' Mallory shouted. 'And in one piece preferably!'

'You can say that again, sir,' Robson said between gritted teeth, swerving to avoid a gaping hole in the track and coming very close to that appalling drop to the valley below. Behind him, Bahadur groaned again and buried his face into his handkerchief, his shoulders heaving.

Now the track was descending. To his front, Mallory could glimpse the bright green of the vineyards clinging to the slope; by his reckoning they couldn't be far from the country road they had left half an hour before. Farmers were notoriously lazy, especially in the South of France with its oppressive heat; they wouldn't move out too far from their villages to tend the land on a day like this. They were going to make it.

'*Sir!*' Robson shrieked. '*Look!*' The young Marine's face contorted with horror, his eyes bulging out of his sweat-lathered face.

Mallory's heart missed a beat.

It was the black Citroen – and it was edging its way out of a small gap cut into the rock wall to their left, its occupants still hidden by that tinted glass. Now it emerged like a sinister black bug, already halfway across the track. And the Renault would slam right into the bigger car unless Robson braked the very next instant.

But Robson didn't brake. Instead he swerved wildly to the right. For one awful, heart-stopping moment, Mallory thought they were going over the side. Later he would swear that the two wheels on his side of the car were stuck out in mid-air. Next moment, they had swerved back on to the middle of the track once more, leaving a small avalanche of boulders and rocks to tumble down to the valley. They had missed going over the precipice by inches – and now the Citroen was racing after them at full pelt.

Desperately Robson floored the accelerator. In the back, the others hung on grimly, wild-eyed and white with fear. Robson took impossible risks, the chassis trembling frighteningly every time he hit another pothole, but the Citroen was steadily gaining on them all the time. Now it seemed to fill the whole road, racing through their wake of dust, its windscreen wipers flailing back and forth furiously, the unseen driver edging his car ever closer.

Then it happened. There was the boom of metal striking metal. The Renault shook violently. Instinctively, Robson hit the brakes and just in time the Citroen driver did the same, as the smaller car once more shimmied perilously close to the edge of the precipice.

'For Chrissake, hold it, man!' Mallory

shrieked, as Robson fought furiously to retain control. A moment later they were back on the road in a cloud of whirling white with the Citroen coming in for another attack.

'They're gonna bumper-jump us right over the side, sir!' Robson gasped, white-knuckled hands hanging onto the wheel grimly, his shirt black with sweat.

'Yes,' Mallory replied. 'That's going to be their accident. They're after–'

The Citroen rammed them again. The men in the back fell into a confused heap with the shock of that terrible impact. Robson's head was whip-lashed from side to side furiously like a metronome. For one terrible moment, Mallory thought he was going to lose control altogether. But in the very last instant he regained charge of the wheel. At the back, Ramsbottom said thickly, 'Bloody hell, I'll never drive in the fast lane again!'

Mallory managed a grin – but only just.

Now the two cars were racing down the steep incline at well over sixty miles an hour, tyres screaming as they cornered, engines howling, both drivers taking impossible risks as they jockeyed for position, each knowing that one of them was going to go over that deadly precipice before they reached the valley floor.

Now Robson was taking the offensive as best he could in the much lighter Renault. Twice he hit the brakes hard, blinding the driver behind him momentarily with the blaze of red brakelight and simultaneously punching the shrill horn. It worked. Both times the unknown driver of the Citroen fell for the dodge. But now he was coming in again to ram the Renault.

This time he changed his tactics. With the advantage on his side, he was careening along, scraping the rock wall and sending up spurts of angry dust and pebble as he tried to strike the Renault's nearside bumper. His intention was obvious. He was going to slam one hell of a blow into Robson's car and send it flying over the edge of the drop.

Mallory rapped out an order. 'Ross, it's us or them. Knock out the rear window!'

'Gie 'em a burst, sir?' Ross cried eagerly, his face set in a sudden wolfish grin of anticipation. 'No mair bluidy pussy-footing?'

'No more bloody pussy-footing!' Mallory cried abov the howl of their racing engine.

'Ay. Got ye, sir!' Ross cried, and squirming round, he rammed his pistol butt against the rear window, while Ramsbottom whipped out his flick-knife and started working on the rubber seal.

'It's not like this in them gangster movies,' Ramsbottom gasped, as he twisted and turned his knife, while behind them the Citroen loomed up ever larger once more, coming round the bend like a bat out of hell.

'Weel, this is no fuckin' gangster movie, mon! This is for fuckin' real!' Ross gasped, and slammed the butt of his machine pistol against the obstinate pane of glass once more.

The Citroen's nose bored into them once more. Mallory gave a gasp of fear as the Renault careened ever closer to the precipice. They seemed to be racing along on the very edge of the drop, sending boulders and rocks pelting downwards at a furious rate. Savagely, the veins standing out at his temples like red cords, Robson fought to keep the car on the road, crying through gritted teeth, 'Come on, you bitch... Come on, hold it!'

With a crash the rear window went. Hot air rushed into the Renault. Ross gave a cry of triumph and started clearing away the shattered remnants with his weapon, while

Ramsbottom clicked home his magazine hastily and, clinging to the seat as best he could, prepared to fire.

Ross beat him to it. Laughing triumphantly, he thrust his muzzle through the window. 'Now, yer foreign buggers, get a load of this!'

In the very same instant that he pressed his trigger, the Citroen slammed into their rear once more. Ross was jolted violently from his firing position. The burst went wild. Missing the racing black car by feet, the slugs ripped up a vicious line of holes the length of the rock face. Angrily he pressed the trigger again. Nothing happened. 'God almighty!' he cursed, and nearly flung the weapon at the other car. 'It's enough to send a mon spare. The bleeder's gone and jammed!'

'Get out of the way, Sarge!' Ramsbottom cried, and elbowed the red-faced, cursing NCO to one side.

'Don't aim for the tyres!' Mallory cried above the roar of the racing motors.

'I know, sir,' Ramsbotton said, taking his aim carefully as if he were back on the range at Poole. 'I'm gonna waste the sod behind the wheel, whoever he is.' His voice thickened as he squeezed one eye closed and prepared to fire.

Wham! The Citroen hit them again. The Renault skidded violently from side to side, Robson fighting the wheel with the last of his strength, sobbing for breath, eyes wild, wide and staring with terror.

'Hold it, Robson!' Mallory cried harshly, his heart thumping madly. 'For God's sake, hold it, man!'

The Renault lurched crazily. For one long, wild second, two of the battered car's wheels were in mid-air and the car seemed about to plunge to its doom far below.

In the rear, Ramsbottom waited, his face showing none of the emotions he felt at that terrifying moment, his whole being concentrated on that black screen only yards away from him, as the unseen driver came in for the kill. For now he had the Citroen exactly where he wanted it – in the outside lane, with his own car close to the rock wall. One more bang like the last one and the Citroen would be over the side. Slowly, Ramsbottom started to take first pressure on his trigger.

At his side Ross tensed. Even Bahadur had forgotten his car sickness. Both of them knew that their lives depended on Ramsbottom's shooting. Now the Citroen edged its way ever closer to the Renault's jagged, battered bumper, and even Ross, unimaginative as he was, could imagine the driver, crouched behind the wheel of the Citroen, beginning to grin in evil anticipation and triumph as he saw the looks of fear on their ashen faces, knowing that in a very few moments they would be dead.

'Hold her steady, young Robson,' Ramsbottom said, his voice icily steady. *'Now!'* He pressed the trigger.

Mallory jumped as the little pistol chattered into violent life and the car was filled with the acrid stink of burnt explosive. For what seemed an age, nothing happened, as a line of gleaming silver holes stitched themselves the length of that sinister black bonnet. Then suddenly the glass shattered in a glistening, blinding spider-web. For the first and last time they caught a glimpse of their unknown assailants, as the runtish, bald-headed man at the wheel, his face contorted with fear, blood streaming down his high forehead, struggled to hold the Citroen on course.

To no avail. Suddenly he flung up his hands as if in despair. That gesture seemed to break the spell. In the Renault Ross gave a great shout of triumph, and Bahadur yelled, *'You banjo 'em, sheeparse. You banjo, mate!*', slapping a suddenly bemused Ramsbottom on the shoulder. Robson hit the brakes, nudging the car tight and close to the rock face in the same moment that the Citroen, filled with screaming men and totally out of control, shot past them, scraping a great silver metallic gouge the length of the Renault. 'Christ, sir, they're going over!' Robson sobbed, as he fought the Renault to a bone-shaking stop. *'They're going over!'*

In open-mouthed awe, they watched as the Citroen teetered on the edge of the precipice, its wheels racing impotently, the trapped men fighting and screaming as they clawed their way to doors that would not open. But only for a moment. Abruptly the edge gave way beneath them. Next instant the Citroen was sailing out into the void. Almost lazily it turned over in mid-air. It struck an outcrop of rock. Tyres burst and shot off independently. There was a great rending of torn metal. Petrol from the split tank sprayed high and ignited immediately in a vivid scarlet flash. Off it sailed again down inexorably to the bottom of the valley. A second later it hit the ground and exploded in a great, echoing roar that seemed to go on for ever.

4

'*Come on, Yuri… Sock it to me… Oh, please, please… More, Yuri, MORE!*' Jo-Jo Johns's desperate plea ended in a groan of ecstasy.

Lying on the bed in his baking hot cabin, a glass of Bourbon in his hand, listening to the sounds coming in through the open porthole and the persistent, steady squeaking of the bed-springs in the cabin nextdoor occupied by Jo-Jo and Bluebeard, Top stifled his own groan just in time. She wasn't faking it; he would have known. She was enjoying it, really *enjoying* having the big Commie dink pushing his goddam red meat into her!

With his free hand, Top wiped the sweat from his brow. He wished he could get drunk this night, but he knew he couldn't. Duty demanded he should stay sober. But he'd really lay one on, a real beaut, once he'd gotten rid of the dink!

He took another swallow of the fierce spirits, trying to wash away his sense of betrayal. He had figured Jo-Jo for a good gal in spite of her profession; whatever she had done, she had done only for the sake of the ole US of A. Hell, he had gotten her all wrong. The Commie dink was giving her what she needed – and she was crying out for more!

Next door, Yuri was grunting in a thick, cruel voice, 'Enough? Enough yet?'

'*No*!' she breathed, and he could just imagine her lying there naked with the Russian fatso towering over her, giving her the full close-up of his blue-veiner, her eyes taking it all in greedily. *'Please don't take it out... Please Yuri*!' Her voice was almost hysterical with pleading now.

'Beg for it,' he heard Yuri command. 'Come now... On your knees! *Down*! *Crawl for it woman*!'

Mad with rage, Top flung his glass at the wall and grabbed for his shoes. He just couldn't stand any more of this. In a minute, he'd haul off and shoot the dink in the nuts, even if they sent him to the slammer for the rest of his born days. He had to get away from them, he just *had* to! He thrust his feet into his shoes savagely and grabbing his jacket, went outside, slamming the door behind him, Jo-Jo's excited whispers and animal cries pursuing him down the corridor.

On deck, he breathed in heavily, savouring the salt tang of the sea and the heady scent of honeysuckle coming from the dark curve of land. From far away came the soft, melodic tinkle of the buoys, as the cruise liner plodded steadily towards Marseilles, her next port of call.

'A penny for them, Top?' A soft voice cut into his angry reverie. He swung round from the rail. It was Ma Barker, who, for once, was without her boys. Perhaps, he told himself maliciously, she had ordered them to bed early to get their beauty sleep, just like the old mother hen she appeared to be.

'Oh, nuthin' much, Ma,' he said, eyeing her as she pulled the knitted shawl tighter around her shoulders, so that she looked like Whistler's mother in bad need of a shave. 'Just be glad to see the end of this mission.'

'The Russian gentleman getting to you, Top?' Ma said, and there was something in the other person's voice which made Top suspect that Ma already knew the answer.

'Something like that, Ma.' Top fought but failed to bottle up his resentment. 'Jesus, Ma, what a cock-eyed world it is! You just don't know where you stand with folk, do ya?'

Ma Barker grinned, showing her yellow teeth, and said quite baldly, 'Well, you know what they say, Top. It takes a stiff rod to catch a big fish!'

Top swallowed hard and gaped, open-mouthed like a village yokel. The words did not seem to go at all with Ma's usual prim and proper attitude. 'What... *What* did ya say, Ma?'

'Don't worry, Top,' Ma said, and laughed. 'I'm not flipping my lid. You heard right. Poor Top, the world must seem a pretty confusing place to you these days, mustn't it?' There was no condescension in Ma's voice, just sympathy.

'You can roger that, Ma,' Top said with feeling. 'Nobody is what they seem to be no more. Everybody's screwed up, got a hang-up of some kind of other.'

Ma continued to smile. 'Including me?'

Top shrugged, but didn't reply. From below came the sound of drunken laughter and a burst of Russian accordion music. This night the 'amateur' crew were entertaining the West German passengers, though Top knew half of them were professional performers. Somewhere a drunken German was singing the *Horst Wessel Lied*.

'I was at the Point, you know. Yes – old

Woo Poo itself. I went because it was the straightest place on earth in those days. Changed a lot since,' Ma added a little wistfully, looking at the moon's rays shimmering on the still, dark water.

'You – at the Point?' Top stuttered incredulously.

'Yes, back in the days when you were a hard-core, brown-shoe non-com with the Big Red One. I graduated, too, Top. Went to Korea as a shave-tail second looey and won me the Silver Star. After that I resigned from the Army. It was the wise thing to do for people like me in those days. I could have ended in Leavenworth. Then I became the other me – the person you and your kind call Ma Barker...'

'It's only a joke, Ma,' Top said hastily, telling himself that the whole goddam world had gone ape. Now Ma Barker was telling him she was a graduate of the Academy and had won the goddam Silver Star. Wow!

'I know, Top. From the movie, isn't it?' Ma threw up her right shoulder in the female manner. 'Though I really don't think I look like that particular individual. No matter. I'm just trying to explain that because people do things that you personally don't approve of – perhaps even can't begin to

214

understand – it doesn't mean that they're complete weirdos or disloyal Americans.' Ma looked hard at a bewildered Top in the silver glow of the moonlight. Down below the Russians had the Germans singing the *Internationale*; obviously the Germans thought it was some kind of Christmas carol. 'I know what's bugging you about Jo-Jo and friend Bluebeard. But whatever she likes about what he's giving her, it doesn't alter her attitude. She'll turn him in at the end of the ride. Nor does the fact that I am as I am mean that I'm not a one hundred percent loyal American. She and I will both do the job we've come here to do, just as poor straight old Mr Ed Gilmour will. Do you read me, Top?'

Ma's voice fell, and suddenly the tall, gaunt person opposite him laid a hand on his. For once Top wasn't appalled. He didn't even feel foolish standing here holding hands with some kind of weirdo fruit who wore women's clothes and an inflatable bra. 'Yeah, I'm reading you, Ma,' he said. 'Affirmative. But I don't think I like this Jo-Jo and Bluebeard thing overmuch.'

Ma chuckled. 'Top, I think you're jealous, you old dog. Didn't know you had it in you.'

'Well, to be frank, Ma, after you've spent

half a lifetime killing dinks, dinks coming through the goddam wire, dinks in the bush, dinks in the paddy, well a guy doesn't take too kindly to some Commie dink slipping it to an American girl. Just can't swallow it, Ma. Sorry,' he ended a little helplessly.

Ma smiled understandingly and patted his hand. 'Forget it, Top. It'll soon be over – then you guys of the CIA can safely lock him away in the wilds and debrief him for the next million years and that'll be the end of any funny business between him and Miss Johns.' Suddenly Ma let go of Top's hand and was her old prissy WASP self. Pulling the shawl a little closer around her skinny yellow shoulders, she said, 'Now to business. Tomorrow evening we dock at Marseilles. On no account is Bluebeard to leave the ship – point one. Point two: you are not to leave his side. Advise Miss Johns accordingly. Point Three: I and my boys will be watching the decks and the gangways discreetly. In short, I want a nice discreet security net drawn tightly about Bluebeard. Clear?'

'Affirmative.'

'Now, there's the question of the Russian crew, Top.' Ma Barker paused and frowned. 'I still haven't been able to discover who's the KGB man on board.'

'I thought it was the radio operator for a while,' Top said guardedly. 'I figured he'd be in a position to communicate with the outside world without arousing suspicion. But he's laying – sorry, he's having sexual intercourse with that blond kid who serves behind the bar. I guess,' he ended lamely, 'the KGB wouldn't go in for that kind of thing, eh?'

Ma grinned a little wickedly. 'You'd be surprised, Top, you'd be surprised!' Then her grin vanished as quickly as it had come. 'Obviously the word is out by now that Bluebeard has defected. Moscow *must* know! The usual routine, as you well know, is to alert all likely exit ports, airports and the like. Soon, I guess, the Russians'll start getting it together and figure that one fat, heavy-drinking KGB agent in Bulgaria is the same fat, heavy-drinking West German who boards a cruise ship on the Black Sea – especially when they find that both were escorted by an exceedingly nubile and obliging American lady. So, I'd give us another forty-eight hours before the KGB on this ship gets the word and by then we've got to have Bluebeard off the *Varna*.'

Top sucked his teeth. 'Ya know, Ma,' he

said slowly, face worried, 'it seems to be taking the dinks a darned long time altogether.'

'What do you mean, Top?'

'Well, the dinks ain't *that* slow. They should have gotten on the stick quicker than this. Come to think of it, we're still on Commie territory.'

'The ship?'

'Yeah.' Top looked around the moonlit deck of the cruise-liner, with the drunken singing coming from below. 'Until we reach French territorial waters, we're still technically in Russia! Hell, if anything went wrong, they could quietly dump us over the side and no one could do a darn thing about it.'

Ma Barker shuddered suddenly and pulled the shawl tighter round her shoulders. 'Don't even think about it, Top,' she said. 'You and me, Top, are survivors – winners. We're both going to live to collect our pensions, aren't we?' She gave a shrill laugh, but there was little warmth in it.

Top hesitated. Somehow he could never see himself on the beach at Fort Lauderdale, drinking suds all day, with nothing to do but watch the fat-assed blue-rinses flaunting their fading charms and the New York hebes playing checker-board underneath the palms – no, sir. 'Guess you're right, Ma,' he said finally.

'Of course I am, Top,' Ma gave a delicate little yawn, patting her painted lips with her hands as if she were ashamed of revealing her teeth. 'Think I'll call it a day, Top. See if my boys are all safely tucked in for the night.' Ma gave what she thought was a silvery woman's laugh. 'They're going to need their beauty sleep for tomorrow. Goodnight, Top.'

'Goodnight, Ma.'

For a moment or two he watched as Ma Barker sauntered down the deck towards the cabins, then he turned back to the still, moonlit sea, his face pensive. Everything was screwed up, the whole goddam world...

Any belief he might once have had that there was a scheme to things had vanished in Nam. One by one the men who had gone out with him had been killed, and somehow he had been able to form each violent death into some kind of lesson. First there had been the bitter irony of the man who was shot by a sniper on the very day his wife gave birth to their first son... Then there was the John Wayne, who should have survived mayhem and murder for ever, just like the movie actor, but who instead had his guts shot out storming a Cong strong-point... The team's star trackman, who had both legs blown off by a mine... But when he had collected all the lessons together, what had they added up to? The answer had been: *nothing*! Now all that kept him going in this crazy, purposeless world, filled with people, even his own associates, whom he could never even come close to under-standing, was the knowledge that he was serving the cause of the good ole US of A. That was all.

For a moment or two more, he stared out across the silent-running sea, the noise from below muted now, almost vanished. 'Oh, *fuck it!*' he cursed softly. He shrugged. Who the fuck cared anyway? He turned and walked back slowly to his cabin, his broad, honest shoulders bowed as if in defeat.

'*Horoscho,*' said Sergei, the radio observer, and turned off the powerful electronic device that could bug virtually every part of the SS *Varna*. He wiped the sweat off his face and turned to Yuri, his lover and superior. 'Oh, fuck it,' he said in English and then in Russian. 'Oh, fuck it indeed!' He laughed, and opposite him, his face glazed with sweat – for the little radio shack, sealed off from the rest of the ship with not even the captain being allowed to enter without Yuri's permission, was stiflingly hot – Yuri laughed with him easily, well satisfied with the way things were going up to now.

'Do you wish for me to report, Yuri?' the radio operator asked, his gaze deferential in spite of the fact that they were lovers. Yuri was not a man to cross; he had a savage temper and excellent connections.

'No,' the younger man said slowly, twirling a stubborn lock of his blond curls unconsciously, as was his habit when he was thinking. 'There is no need to burden the *centrale* with more information. Let's keep the lines clear, in case of emergency,' he said thoughtfully. 'All is going well. The English are being taken care of. The Americans suspect nothing.' He smiled contemptuously at Sergei, who was dabbing his sweat-glazed face with a handkerchief soaked in cheap Cologne. 'What innocents they are, with their Yankee dollars and cheap women!' He hawked harshly and spat expertly into the brass spitoon at Sergei's feet.

Sergei flushed slightly. The gesture indicated contempt not only for the Americans, but also for himself. Yuri was a coming man. If this operation went off successfully, which it surely would, they would part. Yuri would go back to Moscow and that would be that. If they met again in a year's time, Yuri would appear not even to know him. It was always that way in the KGB. Senior ranks never mixed with lower ones; it was worse than a Red Army Mess.

'Do we listen to *him* now?' Sergei asked, indicating a long-range bugging device that could use even an ordinary house window as a bug. By means of electronics, the glass could be employed as a way of listening to everything that went on inside at a range of up to 150 metres.

'No,' Yuri decided, 'let him enjoy his honeymoon a little longer. Soon, I fear, it will be over for good.' He looked significantly at the radio operator and gave him that beautiful even, white-toothed smile of his.

Sergei's heart skipped a beat. Yuri was a wonderful lover. After all, he had been trained in it at that remote school, staffed with whores, male and female, in Leningrad. Often he boasted he could make a 3,000-year-old Egyptian mummy have an orgasm, given time.

'Tonight?' he asked in a trembling voice.

'*Nyet!*' Yuri said, and shook his blond head

firmly. 'Not tonight. Tomorrow is a busy day for us. At Marseilles, just as the Americans, we must be on our guard every minute we are in port. Now we cannot afford to make the slightest of mistakes.' He crooked a finger at the obviously disappointed radio operator. *'Davai,'* he commanded.

Obediently Sergei crept into Yuri's open arms. 'Another forty-eight hours, my little pigeon,' Yuri crooned, stroking Sergei's long black hair, 'and then we can relax. Then,' he pressed his lips softly on Sergei's head, 'we shall have a little honeymoon, all cares forgotten. Now what do you say to that?'

Sergei, kneeling there on the cabin floor, looked up at him, his eyes suddenly brimming with tears, for he was naturally a very emotional man. 'Oh, Yuri, that would be ... wonderful... Absolutely wonderful!'

Yuri grinned in that confident, boyish manner of his.

'There you are, then. That's a promise.' He patted Sergei's head once more and rose to his feet. 'Now I must be off and help the crew to get those drunken Fritz sots back to their cabins so that they can puke the place full by morning.' He shook his head, his good mood suddenly vanished. 'Why do we need their filthy Fritz Marks? Why, indeed?'

And then he was gone, banging the cabin door behind him in sudden anger.

Outside, the spectral moon began to disappear. The clouds veered. Slowly but surely the wind started to change. The *mistral* was beginning to blow. A storm was in the offing.

As the last of the West German tourists staggered back to their cabins, some still singing, others hastening to the toilets to be sick, the SS *Varna* commenced rocking, as that shrill wind started to howl through the superstructure. The first drops of rain pattered down and exploded on the gleaming white deck in stars of black wetness.

In their cabins, those who were already asleep tossed uneasily and tugged up their blankets as it grew colder. Those who were awake frowned apprehensively as the ship began to roll. One or two of the more sober hastily swallowed anti-sea sickness tablets to ward off what was surely to come. A few couldn't sleep at all and would remain awake for the rest of this night. They lay in their swaying beds, staring, as if mesmerised, at the rippling white metal ceiling above them, while outside the wind keened and wailed like a lost soul.

Ma Barker was one such unfortunate. Ma lay there motionless in the tight bunk, stretched out like a dead person in a coffin, mocked by the lively jig played by the inflated white bra hanging from the chair next to the bunk, as it trembled back and forth like a live thing. Top was another, stretched fully clothed save for his shoes, eyes wide open but seeing nothing, smoking, smoking, smoking. Jo-Jo was awake, too. She was sexually exhausted. Still she couldn't sleep, and she didn't know why. Was it the storm outside? The wild rocking of the boat? Or was it apprehension, fear of the morrow?

She turned to her lover. Bluebeard was sprawled halfway across the sweaty, stained rumpled sheets, snoring heavily. She stared at his fat, jowly face in the dim, shaking light. At that moment, the Russian looked like a man well-satisfied with life, a man without a conscience, without problems. For a while she continued to stare down at him, supporting her head with her hand, elbow propped up by the pillow, listening to his easy, regular snoring. 'Lucky sonuva-bitch!' she whispered. Then she lowered her pretty face to her bit of the pillow and tried to sleep. The *mistral* blew on...

BOOK FIVE

Shoot-Out

'For anyone who is tired of life, the thrilling life of a spy should be the very finest recuperator.'

Lord Baden Powell

1

The big thirty-ton British truck rolled down the *autoroute* effortlessly tailing the long line of family cars heading into Marseilles, with the throb and beat of hard rock coming from its cab.

Outside, the green, lush countryside of the South of France was smudged by the pouring rain, and the wipers were ticking back and forth full-out to clear the glass of the heavy *mistral* rain. Not that the rain worried the occupants of the cab much. They munched huge sandwiches and drank beer from cans which they threw out of the side windows at regular intervals, regardless of those cursing French drivers who were rash enough to overtake the monster in this terrible weather.

A couple of times, cars overtook the British truck with its huge twin Union flags on the tail and the letters *'GB'* picked out in bright yellow paint, and pushed into the line just in front of it, to receive a frightening blast on the truck's multiple horns and an angry flash of headlights that bore down on the unfortunate driver in front like baleful, monstrous, white eyes.

Now Marseilles started to loom up out of the *mistral*, as the low black clouds zipped fast across the ragged, swaying trees and the thunder growled like heavy gunfire heard from a long way away. *Péage à 800 metres!*, the warning sign for the toll-gate up ahead, flashed by in the deluge, and there was a flurry of activity among the young men crowded in the steamed-up cab. Horns honking furiously, the British truck cut through a line of family cars and headed for the toll-gate reserved for trucks, followed by shaking fists and cries of '*Sales cons anglais!*', which were met with equally raucous cries of '*Up yer kilt, Frog!*' from the truck. As the truck braked at the toll-gate in a wake of white flashing water, some humorist called, 'D'yer take Co-op stamps, mate?' and a handful of grubby notes were thrust into the keeper's outstretched hand. Even before the light had changed from red to green again, the truck's air-brakes hissed once more and it was rolling forward into the shabby suburbs of the great French port, empty cans of Long Life sailing towards the ragged Algerians who peopled this area, accompanied by coarse demands to 'Get off the street, Paki! This is white man's country, mate!'

Crouched in the cavernous back of the trailer, Mallory shook his head in wonder. Ramsbottom, Robson and Ross were playing their new-found role all too well. He only hoped they didn't get picked up by the law before they reached the docks. Still, they were doing a commendable job of being obnoxious Brits, full of working-class piss and vinegar – and not a little beer. Who would take them for the professionals of the SBS?

He handed the photo of Bluebeard to Bahadur, who was squatting in the seat of the battered mini-moke, with the evil-smelling trash cans in the back and the Marseilles plates. 'That's our man, Bahadur. Study his face well. I don't want you to forget it. Clear, Rifleman?'

'Yes, sir,' Bahadur said, taking the photograph delicately and staring at it intently as if his whole life depended upon it, as the truck began to slow with the thickening traffic.

In the last twelve hours since that hair-raising chase in the hills, everything had gone completely according to plan. They

231

had abandoned the smashed-up Renault outside Montelimar and tramped into Montelimar Nord, where, just outside the *autoroute* motel complex, the truck had been waiting for them in the truck park. The key had been where they had been told it would be: attached to the chassis by a magnetic clip. The clothes had been stowed away waiting for them, too: typical workmen's donkey-jackets, complete with a rash of plastic Union badges, and overalls. Hidden in the back with the mini-moke, there had been the money, extra food, and the customs documents for the truck, certifying that it had left Dover and entered France at Calais on its way to Marseilles to pick up a cargo of Algerian fruit, imported into the EEC under the terms of France's special arrangement with her former colony. Nothing had been overlooked. Even the beer was right: English lager and brown ale from Newcastle. As far as the average French customs man was concerned, they were typical English long-distance lorry drivers, equipped with the usual duty-free whisky and cartons of cigarettes to ease their path through any border post that was proving to be too slow for them and their cargo of perishable fruit. There was only one

232

difference. To the rear of the big truck, the refrigeration compartment didn't function. Instead, it had been transformed into a mobile cell, complete with straitjacket and its own elsan sanitary bucket; for it would be there that – hopefully – Bluebeard would make his twenty-four-hour journey in the sealed-and-bonded truck back to Dover.

Mallory gave Bahadur a few more moments, before he said, 'Well, Rifleman, this is how we're going to do it. Once we've entered the commercial docks with the pass that they've provided us with from London, Marine Robson parks. We – that is, Sergeant Ross, Corporal Ramsbottom and you and I – leave in the trash cart.' He indicated the little open vehicle with corrugated sides, which smelt pungently of rotten vegetables and other waste.

Bahadur nodded his understanding.

'Now, the Russians lean over backwards to observe every possible Western European rule and regulation. They don't want to lose the foreign currency that these cruises of theirs bring in. Therefore, unlike most skippers, their captains don't simply dump waste overboard. In our latitudes they're very concerned about pollution, so they've contracted for their waste to be removed at every port they call at. We're the contractors for Marseilles. It's the ideal way for us to penetrate the *Varna*. Undoubtedly they'll be watching the main exits and entrances, but I doubt if they'll be guarding the waste-disposal point.'

Again Bahadur nodded, as Mallory rose to lift the pile of bright blue, zip-fastened overalls of the type worn by French workers from the corner, and pulling out an overall, tossed it to the little brown man.

'Now, when we come out again, we won't be carrying trash in that middle can,' he continued, selecting an overall for himself and pulling it on, while Bahadur did the same. 'God willing, we'll be carrying Mister Bluebeard in person.'

'But what if trouble, sir?' Bahadur asked, completing his disguise by perching on his head one of those grey woolly caps that only Algerian workers seemed to wear. 'Banjo Bluebeard?'

Mallory frowned, as if the other man had just reminded him of something unpleasant. 'There will be *no* trouble, Bahadur,' he said firmly, after a moment's thought. 'The plan doesn't allow for it. We must find him in his cabin, inject him with the tranquilliser and speed him on his way before he knows

what's hit him, into that evil-smelling con-
tainer over there.'

'And this lady here?' Bahadur asked, tapping a picture of Jo-Jo Johns which Mallory
had also given him first to study.

'She stays where she is.'

'Pity, sir.' Bahadur grinned evilly, dark
eyes sparkling. 'She oil my truncheon any
day.'

Mallory shook his head in mock-wonder.
Where the devil did Bahadur pick up such
phrases? 'She's not oiling anybody's truncheon, Rifleman, thank you very kindly.
This is going to be a very quick snatch-and-
skedaddle op. If anyone tries to stop you,
belt them – but do it quietly. Clear?'

Bahadur looked longingly at his *kukri*,
resting in its gleaming leather case in the
corner, but he said dutifully enough. 'Yes,
sir. Belt very quietly.'

'Sir!'

Mallory turned hastily to see Robson
peering through the canvas at the back of
the cab. To his front, the windscreen wipers
hissed back and forth furiously, sending the
raindrops flicking off in white anger. 'Yes?'

'Coming to the dock gate now, sir. There's
fuzz of some kind.'

'Dockyard police. If there's any hassle,

give them a carton of Benson and Hedges.'

'Sir.' Hastily Robson thrust back the flap as the truck slowed down and stopped.

For a moment or two there was no sound save the hiss of the rain and the steady throb of the big diesel engine. Someone said something in French which Mallory couldn't quite catch. Then Ramsbottom, as imperturbable as ever, said in his thickest Yorkshire accent, 'Happen yer right, mate. But I don't hold with it... Here, have yersen a smoke. Real English fags. None o' yer Continental muck.'

Mallory groaned silently. Why couldn't the English ever stop putting their foot in it on the Continent? Either they praised everything to excess, or condemned it out of hand as foreign and therefore no good. For them the wogs began at Calais.

'*Passez... Allez!*' said a bored, grumpy voice, and Ramsbottom at the wheel thrust home first gear noisily. Next to him, Ross grunted. 'Typical, ain't it? Allus holding out their bluidy palms to be greased. Cannae trust any o' them.'

As they started to roll again, from some way off Mallory could hear the chatter and snort of a shunter engine. They were inside the docks. He flashed a quick look at the green-glowing dial of his watch in the gloom of that cavernous interior. They had exactly two hours and ten minutes before the SS *Varna* was due to dock.

Now the blue-and-white ferry from Algeria had docked, and the shabby Algerians were scurrying through the driving rain for cover, their bundles held over their heads, while from the bowels of the ship, the containers were being dragged out by the forklifts. All was haste and anger; in Marseilles they weren't used to rain.

Yuri lowered his glasses. The rain would keep away sightseers, and only a handful of Fritzes were going ashore to see the port. Now they crowded around the exit, dressed in plastic macs, shouting to each other in warning, '*Pass doch auf, Otto. Die sind alle Gauner hier... Ich hab' mein Geld versteckt... Du auch?... Wir schauen uns nur die Altstadt an und dann kommen wir sofort zurück...*'

Yuri stared at them for a few moments, his handsome face set in a look of contempt. Were these the same people who had reached the gates of Moscow in the winter of '41? It seemed hardly possible that these fat grey men, fussy, pompous, laden with gold and flashy jewellery, could be the same grim, grey-clad soldiers who had struck such fear into the heart of his parents' generation so long ago.

He dismissed them and thrusting up his collar, sprinted easily down the rain-drenched deck, well aware of the admiring gazes of the fat Fritz women inside the lounge. He could have had any one of them at the crook of his finger, he knew, and be well paid for it, too. But soon that business would be over. He vaulted lightly up the stairs that led to the radio shack. After this op, his promotion would come and his life had to develop in a more serious fashion, as befitted a senior KGB officer.

As he flung open the door, the radio operator's admiration was only too clear. He dropped everything immediately, his stupid calf's-eyes full of love. 'All right,' Yuri snapped, 'we're about to dock. I've checked the quay. It's almost deserted. This shit-weather is keeping it clear, fortunately.'

'Yes, Yuri, and the forecast is heavy showers and Force Eight winds for the next twenty-four hours.'

'*Horoscho*.' Yuri nodded his approval. 'Exactly right. In twenty-four hours it'll be all over.'

The radio operator's face lit up excitedly.

'And then we shall have time for ourselves, won't we, Yuri!' He reached out his soft white hand, as if to take Yuri's.

The latter snatched it out of the way. '*Da, da,*' he said hurriedly.

'*Kak shal!*' the radio operator said a little sulkily.

'There'll be time for that later,' Yuri snapped, very businesslike, his light-blue eyes hard and efficient. 'Right. Get on with it now. You watch his cabin and the Yankees. None of them are going ashore by the way, so there should be no problems.' He laughed contemptuously. 'Probably the big grey one will get drunk – that is what his kind always do on days like this. As for the other one...' He shrugged contemptuously. 'Heaven knows what his kind get up to.'

'And you, Yuri?'

'I shall patrol the deck. At this stage of the game, we cannot afford the slightest slip-up, Sergei.'

'But it's very wet,' the radio operator protested. 'You must wear your raincoat...'

Yuri shot him a lethal look. 'Trap!' he barked harshly. 'Now get on with it – *davai!*'

For a moment it seemed as if the radio operator might burst into tears – he could never stand harshness from Yuri. But he pulled himself together just in time and reached for his peaked cap.

'*Horoscho*,' Yuri said in approval, telling himself what a weak sister Sergei really was. If he had the privileges of certain KGB men, he knew, he would have Sergei eliminated in due course. One never knew. People like Sergei might prove an embarrassment to him in later life. 'I'm going now.'

Opening the door of the shack, he disappeared into the heavy rain.

Ma Barker watched him go, eyes narrowed against the beating raindrops blown in by the wind squalls. Top was probably right in a way. It wasn't the radio operator, although he was part of the scheme of things; it was the blond queer. Up there in the radio shack was officer country. What would a lowly bar steward be doing up there, dishing out orders to an officer, unless he was a KGB man? The dinks were even more rank-conscious than West Point. Yeah, Ma Barker told herself, the blond queer was the *Varna*'s KGB officer, and the radio operator was his subordinate – the one who kept him in touch with the *centrale*. That was how it worked, just as Top had half-suspected.

'Leroy,' she commanded.

One of her boys, wrapped in an expensive white Burberry, detached himself from the shadow of the overhanging lifeboat. 'Sir?' He blushed. 'I mean, Ma?'

'Watch the radio operator. He's one of them. I'll take the blond one. All right?'

'Yes. Yes, ma'am.' The boy's blush deepened even more, and Ma smiled winningly at him. He was such an innocent.

'Then, off you go. And Leroy?'

'Sir – Ma'am?' he stopped in his track, stuttering with confusion.

'Change that coat soon, will you? You look like Bogart playing some character from Chandler.'

Top watched too. The device was primitive, he knew, and he'd feel an awful asshole if anyone came into the cabin and caught him at it. But it was effective. As he stood there in the shower, upturned tooth-glass pressed against the metal bulkhead that separated him from Bluebeard's cabin, he could hear virtually everything they said and did. And as he listened he felt his blood boil with anger again. The Commie slopehead dink was trying to get her back into the hay again! Top felt his big hand shake with anger

241

as he heard those little half-suppressed gasps, whispers, laughs as Jo-Jo's clothes were removed one by one with excited, clumsy hands. Soon, godammit, they'd be practising the goddam two-backed, four-legged beast *again*!

2

Crouched and bent against the pelting rain, heavy refuse drums raised as if to protect their heads from the heavy downpour, the four of them advanced from the mini-moke towards the ship. Behind them, Robson had just edged the truck around the side of the port authority building, and, leaving the engine running, had clambered out to examine the tarpaulin, as if he wasn't quite satisfied that his cargo was properly roped down. No one took any notice of him. It was too wet, and the windows of the building streamed with raindrops like sombre, cold tears.

In the lead, the collar of his blue overalls turned up and his hands dug firmly into his pockets, a cigarette glued to his bottom lip in what he fondly hoped was a good imitation of a typical French worker, Mallory eyed the open side of the *Varna*. It was truly the 'tradesmen's entrance' to the ship, he told himself: bottles, cans, sacks of refuse piled up everywhere under the dim yellow light, and somewhere in the further recesses of the place he could hear a furtive scampering sound which told him that rats were about. But they were the only sign of activity on board. There was no sign of the crew.

Mallory nodded his approval and, wrinkling up his nose as his nostrils were assailed by the stink of stale smoked mackerel and garlic which hung over the place in a pungent cloud, he stepped into the ship cautiously. The others followed and for a few moments pretended to examine the rubbish, like men considering how to spin the assignment out until the rain had stopped. For his part, Mallory orientated himself quickly, recalling the plan of the *Varna* which had been supplied in the MOD's folder.

Bluebeard and the bird had a B-Special Cabin located on the upper deck, port side – which was to the good. As the ship was berthed, it would mean they couldn't be observed from the shore, and if he knew sailors, the crew members would already be in their bunks, getting some shuteye, or tucked away in their own lounge, belting back a few jars and playing cards for money. Sailors were a conservative lot in spite of their calling; they didn't change much over the years. 'All right,' he commanded, 'drop all but the one can and follow me. Let's go.'

'Ye heard the officer,' Ross snarled. 'Get rid o 'em. You can carry the can, Gunga Din.' He laughed coarsely at his own humour.

'Oh, shut up, Ross!' Mallory snapped, and felt for the hypo, filled with tranquilliser. 'Move it.'

Sergeant Ross 'moved it', followed by Ramsbottom, his only weapon one of his own socks hastily filled with wet sand, and Bahadur, lugging the heavy stinking can. Slowly, trying hard to be casual, they entered the warm, smelly bowels of the ship. The operation was underway.

Grinning hugely, Bluebeard levered himself up from the rumpled bed, while Jo-Jo, completely naked save for her black stockings which he had insisted she keep on – 'We Russians are old-fashioned in our eroticism.' – lay there exhausted, her hair matted to her head with sweat. 'I go for champagne,' grunted the Russian, slipping into his trousers and pulling on a thin plastic raincoat. 'Now we must have champagne.'

'Sure,' she said lazily, hardly raising her

head. Now she felt really drowsy; now she could sleep. 'Take your time, Yuri. There's no mad rush.'

Bluebeard slipped into his shoes and turned up his collar against the rain, which was still belting down outside, making a mad drumming sound on the deck. 'Crimean pink. The best,' he said grandly. 'We celebrate tomorrow, eh?'

She yawned luxuriously and her lovely full breasts, the nipples still full and erect, rode up her naked body. Hastily he bent down and nuzzled each nipple playfully. 'Good, eh?' he growled proudly. 'Yuri make love good, eh? All Russian men make love good!'

'Uh-uh,' she agreed with another yawn, as he went out, closing the door hastily against the driving rain. Jo-Jo shut her eyes. Now she felt she could sleep for a week.

On the other side of the partition, Top relaxed. He placed the tooth-glass back on the shelf in the shower and stepped outside. He needed a drink, too. A stiff one. With a hand that still trembled with a mixture of rage and envy, again attacked by that strange sense of betrayal and let-down, he took a hefty swig of Bourbon – straight from the bottle. Outside, head bent against the rain, the big Russian bastard hurried by the porthole on his way to the duty-free shop to buy his 'Crimean pink, the best'. Top raised his bottle to the passing figure. 'I hope it fucking well chokes you!' he toasted the Russian. 'Chokes you fucking well dead!' He took another hefty slug of the fiery alcohol and it exploded with a satisfying burst of flame in the pit of his stomach. Suddenly Top felt better. Another twenty-four hours and it would be all over. He would be rid of the two of them. Then he'd go on a bender, a real humdinger, the father and mother of a bender; and he wouldn't stop till he knew no more pain. He took another drink. His hands had stopped trembling at last.

They were climbing the long tight companionway from the bowels of the ship, passing the corridors leading off to 'G' deck, where the cheapest cabins were located. Here and there they could hear the muted voices of those tourists who had decided not to go ashore. But everything seemed normal. So far they hadn't seen a single crew member, not even a steward summoned by a passenger to take care of some supposed emergency or other. Mallory reasoned that his surmise had been correct. The crew members were bedding down for the afternoon before the evening sailing and dinner.

'When we get to the top,' he whispered to the others mounting the steep stairs behind him, 'we'll split up. You, Ross and Ramsbottom, together. I'll take Bahadur with me. Okay?'

Behind him, Bahadur, lugging the heavy steel can, his dark face glazed with sweat, nodded his understanding, and Ross and Ramsbottom raised their thumbs in the sign of agreement.

'We'll close on his nib's cabin from two sides and–'

'*Sto*?' a gruff voice inquired in Russian.

Mallory spun round. In the corridor running to the right, a big man in a dirty singlet stood there with a wrench in one hand, a brown leather workman's satchel of tools in the other. For a moment Mallory was speechless.

The big Russian looked at him and then down at the others crowding the steps behind Mallory and repeated his query. '*Sto*?' He shrugged and added. '*Ne ponye- mayu po russki*?'

Mallory shook his head helplessly. He had indeed studied Russian, but at this particular moment he couldn't even remember the word for 'No.'

'*Tu es les ordures, oui, copain?*' the Russian plumber – for that was what he seemed to be from his tools – said in broken, heavily accented French. '*Que tu veux ici, eh?*'

'*Les ordures, bouteilles, conserves,*' Mallory stuttered, eyeing the man, already aware that he wasn't being believed.

'*Par içi,*' the Russian said, wagging his wrench at them. '*Par ici, là bas. Compris, copain? Allez vite!*' he advanced on Mallory, hands extended in a shooing gesture, as if to physically usher them down to the hold again.

Mallory made a snap decision. It was now or never. He dived forward at the big man. His shoulder caught the Russian in the chest. He gave a harsh gasp, as the air was knocked out of his lungs. But to Mallory's surprise he didn't go down. Instead, he staggered a few paces and almost immediately lunged forward, dropping his wrench as he did so, jabbing his outstretched fingers right at Mallory's face, using the old sailors' brawl trick of trying to blind his opponent.

Mallory dodged the cruel blow in the very last instant. He clasped the Russian to him, nostrils assailed by the sudden stink of male sweat and garlic. At once he buried his face into the man's hairy chest to prevent him trying the blinding trick again. With his free hand he sought the Russian's brawny neck.

'Christ, let me get at him,' Ramsbottom hissed, jockeying for position in the tight confines of the corridor. 'Gimme a chance, sir, please.'

'Built like a brick shithouse. Need *kukri*!' Bahadur suggested, eyes rolling, as the Russian grunted and brought up his knee.

Mallory blocked it and winced with pain as their knees struck. The Russian, he told himself grimly, needed no training in unarmed combat. He had learned all the dirty tricks he needed to know in waterfront dives the world over.

The Russian lunged again, while Ramsbottom hovered back and forth on his toes like a referee at a boxing match, searching for an opportunity to land a blow with the sand-filled sock on the man's greasy-locked head. Thrusting up his brawny, hairy arms, he tried to break the hold that Mallory had on his throat. It was the wrong move. Mallory let go. The Russian stumbled blindly forward, caught off-balance by the surprise withdrawal. Mallory didn't give him a second chance. He crooked his arm round the Russian's neck from the back. He jerked it back. Instantly the blood supply was cut off and the Russian's face was flushed a violent crimson. Feet astride, eyes bulging with the effort, veins standing out like red chords at his temples, Mallory exerted all his strength.

'That's the way, sir!' Ross hissed, eyes flashing up and down the corridor to check if this desperate struggle to the death had been observed. 'Squeeze the life out of the Commie bugger!'

Now the Russian thrashed and gasped, wriggling frantically to escape that vice-like lethal hold. Mallory held on for all he was worth, the sweat streaming down his face in rivulets, threatening to blind him at any moment. The Russian grunted. He made one last desperate attempt to break loose. Mallory hung on grimly, tugging his arm ever closer. Abruptly the strength went from the Russian. His body went limp suddenly and he hung there lifelessly, held upright only by Mallory's grip. For one long moment Mallory held on fighting for control, his legs feeling like indiarubber. Then, slowly and very gently, he lowered the Russian to the deck. 'Poor brave bugger,' he whispered.

Then they were off in a hurry. There was

no time to lose now. They had to nobble Bluebeard and be off with him before the alarm was raised – and that wouldn't be far off now...

Happy in spite of the pouring rain, the two large Vodkas which he just drunk in rapid succession warming his enormous girth, Bluebeard left the lounge, a double magnum of Champagne clutched in his fat paw, the wind whipping his clothes about his body as the *mistral* came howling in straight off the sea. But Yuri Serov didn't feel the wind or the rain. Things were going too well for him to be worried by such trivia. Now that he was freed of the responsibilities of office, life had become like one long, marvellous holiday. He had money, he had time, he had the woman: a woman who was far more sophisticated in her love-making than any he had known back in the Homeland. Naturally they would take her off him in due course, when he reached the United States. It was to be expected. But there would be others, many of them, even if they were only the paid whores that the CIA had running for them. He smiled to himself, as he fought his way back against the howling wind. After all, gash is gash, he whispered to himself. What did it matter if a woman was a whore? Pay her and get her to perform. Most times they were better than those who had to be wined and dined before they would spread their legs.

He paused to catch his breath and held onto a stanchion. A few metres away, his tail stopped too, and in the dripping mirror of the lounge window, he could see his image, soaked and miserable, as he ducked for the protection of one of the lifeboats. Bluebeard grinned. The little queer deserved to get soaked. How people could enjoy men when there were women – great juicy women with silky-white flanks and tits like melons – was beyond him!

He clutched his bottle tighter and pushed on, the sudden rain squall beating him a physical blow across the face. It didn't bother him. Not even the *mistral* could spoil his mood this day. He'd spend the rest of it in bed with Jo-Jo. How he loved it when she crawled, naked, on her knees to him, begging – no, *pleading* for it, waiting like a dog for him to use her anyway he damn well pleased, backwards, sidewards, upside-down...

He paused again, gasping for breath. He was getting far too fat. These days, it took him all of five, heartpounding, choking minutes just to do up his own shoes. Still, his shortage of breath hadn't affected his performance in bed. And how the American woman loved it! Was it because American men were too sophisticated? Too effete? Pecker in the head instead of between the legs, where it should be? Could that be it? He chuckled at the thought. Top came to mind. The big grey-haired CIA man certainly fancied the plump little pigeon Jo-Jo. You didn't need a crystal ball to see that. How the American hated him! More likely than not, Top could hear the little games he and Jo-Jo played through the thin wall of the cabin. He chuckled again; he hoped it would make him suitably envious again when he and Jo-Jo got to it once more after they'd drunk the bubbly. He'd make her cry out all right this evening! Warmed by that pleasant thought, he set off again.

But not for long.

A scruffy brown shape emerged from the gloom. The creature looked like one of those niggers found employed in all these western ports as cheap labour, doing the jobs their white comrades refused to do. Holding up a cigarette in a skinny brown hand, the man

254

made as if to strike a match with his other.

'A light? *Tu veux feu?*' Bluebeard asked in his poor French. Normally he wouldn't waste time on such miserable scum, but in his present mood he could afford to be generous. With his free hand he fumbled in his dripping raincoat for his matches.

A sudden noise alerted him to his danger. Too late! He spun round – just as the sock filled with sand descended on his skull like a hammer. His knees gave way immediately and he crumpled straight into Mallory's and Ramsbottom's waiting arms.

'*At the double!*' Mallory cried, sinking the needle of the hypo deep into the Russian's blubber, as Bahadur trundled the can out from its hiding place. 'Come on now!'

With a grunt, Ramsbottom heaved the Russian towards the drum. Bahadur and Mallory took Bluebeard's limp legs and pushed forward. Somehow the three of them managed to get the unconscious man inside and, with the drum tilted to one side, began to roll it along the deck to the companionway which led below.

'Hey! Stop! What are you doing?' The radio operator came round the corner and cried in alarm at the sight of these four men in their soaked blue overalls.

'Leave him to me, sir,' Ross growled. He didn't understand the language, but he understood that the stranger spelled trouble. 'I'll fix his ears for him.'

Waving his hands in what he fondly imagined to be a display of gallic fury, Ross reeled off a string of Gaelic, as the radio operator ran towards him through the hissing rain, face wild with fear; for he knew if he had slipped up, there would be all hell to pay.

Ross held his palms outwards like he had seen the Frogs do, as if he were about to explain something. Sergei, pelting after the men with drum, tried to shove the importuning hands to one side, shouting angrily in Russian. It was just what Ross, product of a Gorbals street-gang, had been waiting for: a chance to get his antagonist within striking distance before he realised his intentions. His knee flashed out. It caught Sergei right in the crotch. He gave a fearful scream and went reeling back against the bulkhead, clutching his ruined testicles, strange little bubbling noises coming from deep down within him, mouth gaping wide open like that of a stranded fish.

'Beautiful, mon, absolutely beautiful,' Ross whispered in delight, as the Russian hung there moaning and writhing, hands clasped to his crotch, completely defenceless. Slowly, deliberately, he grasped the man by the throat and held him steady, measuring the distance between himself and the Russian. He hauled back his fist. His light blue eyes glittered with sadistic pleasure. This was going to be fun. After all this time taking crap from the Commie bastards without being able to retaliate because them nancy-boys in Whitehall had forbidden it, he was going to get his own back at last! 'All right,' he hissed through gritted wolfish teeth, 'try this one on for size, mate!'

His fist flashed through the air. It connected squarely with Sergei's chin. Sergei gave one agonised stifled moan. Next moment he was hanging there, dark-red blood spurting from his ears, nose and split lips in a fierce jet.

For one long moment, Ross held him there, savouring the mess he had made of the Russian's face. He certainly wasn't the pretty boy he had been only a moment or so ago. Already his jaw was beginning to swell, and a greenish hue was spreading rapidly across his lower face. 'Got to get up earlier in the day to catch old Ross, mate,' he said triumphantly, and let the unconscious man slide down to the wet deck. Next moment he was pelting through the rain after the rest. They had nobbled Bluebeard at last!

3

Yuri panicked. First there was the dead man in the corridor, obviously violently done to death. Now here was Sergei, lying unconscious in a pool of his own blood, the rain beating down on his back. What was happening? *What was going on?* It was Serov – something to do with Comrade Serov. Instinctively he knew that was what it was. He let Sergei drop back into the pool of blood, trying to fight back an unreasoning wave of fear and apprehension. Perhaps it was one of those Corsican gangs he had heard about – *'L'Union Corse'*, which terrorised this part of France. Petty criminals, looting cabins while the passengers were ashore... It had happened before, he knew.

He stood up, the rain forgotten, and bit his bottom lip. How was he going to check? He couldn't exactly burst open the door of the cabin and demand to know if everything was all right. But what if it wasn't, and he was standing here idly, doing nothing? How would that look back in Moscow? He swallowed hard and calmed himself. He must think of something – *he must*! He wiped the rain from his face and slicked back his hair, already walking to Serov's cabin, forming the words of his enquiry in German; for he knew he mustn't destroy the cover Serov had built up. He was a West German tourist and he had to be addressed in that language. He stopped outside the door of their cabin and pressed his ear to it. No sound came from inside. He considered for a moment. Should he simply open the door or peer in through the window? No, that was out. He'd try a straightforward enquiry. Politely, he tapped on the door. *'Herr Mueller, bitte?'*

For a long moment, there was no answer. Panic gripped him again – then a woman's voice said, *'Ein moment, bitte.'*

He breathed a sigh of relief. It was the American bitch, and from the creak of springs, he judged she was on or in the bed. His handsome face cracked into a worried grin. Serov was at it again. Where *did* the man find all that energy?

The door opened a slit and he caught a glimpse of a sheer black nightdress clutched in a white hand in front of the girl's body.

Obviously she had been sleeping naked.

'*Könnte ich bitte mit Herrn Mueller sprechen*?' he asked in his best German.

'*Herr Mueller*?' she echoed, her face revealing her bewilderment all too clearly. Suddenly she realised what he was saying. '*Herr Mueller*! *Warum wollen Sie denn mit ihm sprechen*?'

'*Ist er da*?' he demanded urgently, his nerve beginning to go again.

She didn't answer. The look of bewilderment in her eyes had changed to one of apprehension now.

'Shit!' Yuri cried in perfect English, losing his calm altogether. 'Where is he? Where is your man?'

'Hey, what *is* all this?' she cried, trying to shut the door in his face. 'Go away or I'll call some–'

She never finished. Pushing on the door with all his strength, he sent her reeling back to fall on the floor, lovely in her nakedness. But Yuri had no eyes for her charms, as she sprawled there on the floor, hair in disorder, legs spread apart. 'Where is he?' he shrieked, beside himself with fear now. Everything was falling apart, descending into the abyss. He didn't intend to go down with it.

'Hell – who are you?' Jo-Jo countered,

knowing now that something – something terrible – had gone wrong with the great escape plan. Why else would this Russian creep, who was supposedly a barman, be barging into her cabin like this, firing questions at her like a man who was accustomed to giving orders – and having them obeyed at double-quick time? 'What goddam right have you to–'

Her words ended in a howl of pain, as Yuri slapped her across the face with his open hand, sending her head swinging to one side. 'I'm asking the questions here, American whore!' he yelled, his face suffused with rage. Viciously he struck her again. Her head slammed back. A thin trickle of blood started to curl from her right nostril and suddenly her eyes were filled with fear. 'Why are you so cruel?' she whispered in a broken voice. 'Why?'

Yuri nodded his head in approval. *Now* the bitch was ready to talk...

Hearing the thin scream, Top dropped the bottle. He knew he was already half-stoned, but he wasn't *that* drunk. That was Jo-Jo next-door – and she had screamed. And this time, it wasn't because the Commie dink was giving her a cheap thrill. *Jo-Jo was in trouble*! Top lumbered to his feet like an enraged elephant, little red eyes suddenly blazing with anger. *No one was going to hurt his Jo-Jo!*

He struggled to the door, suddenly realising just how bombed he was. His fingers felt like thick pork sausages as they fumbled for the door-knob. Somehow he got it open. A blast of rain-laden wind struck him icily in the face. He stood swaying there for a moment, shaking his head and feeling the wind begin to sober him up again. There was the scream again. He forgot his condition. Lumbering clumsy to the next cabin, he wrenched open the door.

Yuri panicked as the drunken giant stumbled inside. Hands outstretched like a wrestler preparing to gouge the eyes out of some unfortunate opponent, the big American advanced upon him, mouthing unintelligible animal obscenities. The American was going to kill him! On the floor, Jo-Jo gasped through the blood and vomit, 'Thank God, Top... *Thank God!*' and began to sob as if her very heart was broken.

Top roared with rage. Yuri tensed, hand fumbling for the inside of his pocket. He would rush him in a moment. There was the flash of steel. As if by magic a flick-knife had appeared in Yuri's hand as he crouched there, waiting.

'*Commie dink!*' Top yelled, and dived forward, arms flailing.

Yuri went reeling back, submerged under Top's huge bulk. Together they slammed to the bulkhead. Somehow Yuri held on to his wickedly sharp knife. Now he thrust it forward into that massive, powerful body. Top gave a gasp. Still he didn't relax his killing hold. Desperately, feeling his strength slipping away from him fast, unconsciousness threatening to overcome him at any moment, he thrust the knife ever deeper. With the last of his strength, as red and silver stars began to explode in the red wavering mist before his eyes, Yuri ripped upwards and upwards, feeling his knuckles flood with hot blood that surged along his arm and continued running, sticky and copper-smelling...

Top wanted to scream, but he had the breath only to howl. He didn't want to, but he couldn't help it. The strength was draining from his body as if an invisible tap had been opened. He was going down. *Down*! There was no sound save his own harsh, hectic breathing. Jo-Jo was staring up at him, screaming, screaming, screaming. But he couldn't hear her. It was as if some monster had thrown glutinous tentacles over his ears to drown out all sound. He felt something wet, hot and slimy edge into his hands. He looked down, slowly, very slowly. His guts were slipping out of his ripped abdomen, greypurple, steaming and obscene like an uncurling snake. He shook his head, as if in disbelief. He couldn't be dying, could he? After all he had survived? *No way*! Lifting his head as if it weighed a ton, he stared at the little Russian. He still crouched there, face wild, knife clutched to his loins like a blood-covered penis. Then he knew. He *was* dying! He'd had it. At last. He tried to smile, but failed miserably. 'Commie,' he gasped, 'Commie di–' And slammed to the floor face forward, dead...

Now the ship's sirens were screaming the alarm. Alpha Team had served long enough on board ship to recognise the signal. Three long, three short blasts on the siren. Everywhere they could hear the crew doubling to their duty stations. And they knew why. They had been discovered, and now the Russians were sealing off the ship!

Desperately, with Bahadur and Ross half-rolling, half-carrying the drum containing Bluebeard's unconscious bulk, they sought a way out. Civilians came bolting down the corridor towards them, the women in their old-fashioned nightdresses, screaming and toothless, struggling into expensive fur coats, jewel-boxes clutched to their shapeless dugs. An old man with one leg hopped out of a cabin to the left, artificial limb clasped under his arm as if it were a parcel, crying in German, 'Don't let a cripple drown, please... *Don't!*' They pushed by him, and Ross, face red and angry with the effort, growled, 'Now we're right in it, up to our necks! They've blown the bluidy whistle on us!'

'Yes, but no reason to panic!' Mallory snapped, as he blundered on in the lead. 'Come what may, they're not going to have any political scandal in a neutral–'

He stopped short. A big man in a dirty white cook's overall came out of the corridor to the right, meat cleaver clasped in his hand. He took in the scene at once. He cursed in Russian and, brandishing his cleaver, rushed them. Next to Mallory, Ramsbottom threw up his sand-filled sock. The cleaver flashed. The sock exploded sand everywhere and Ramsbottom went reeling back, knuckles suddenly flushed scarlet. Mallory acted instinctively. He stamped the heel of his boot down hard on the cook's foot. He howled with pain and faltered for a moment. Mallory didn't give him a chance to recover. Dashing in beneath that terrible cleaver, he butted his head straight into the Russian's face. The man screamed thickly and slammed against the bulkhead, false teeth bulging out of his mouth stupidly, bright white against the thick red jelly of blood. Slowly he started to slide down the metal wall, trailing blood after him, cleaver tumbling from his suddenly nerveless fingers.

Now they were clear of the passenger quarters, and Mallory made a quick decision. 'Into the car deck!' he yelled above the shrill, urgent scream of the siren. 'Come on!' He grabbed at the metal handle of the narrow door to his right and jerked it down. Much to his relief, the door opened and he stumbled into the hold, which was packed with cars, all of them with West German number plates. They were the vehicles of German tourists planning to drive back to the Federal Republic once the cruise ended in Vigo, Northern Spain.

Leaving the others to get the unconscious Bluebeard in his drum through the narrow doorway as best they could, Mallory zig-zagged through the line of gleaming BMWs and Mercedes, praying fervently that the hold-door would be worked by electricity and not the power of the now silent ship's engines...

The captain, pale, shaken, and already almost at the end of his tether, stared wild-eyed at the little blond KGB agent. They stood together on the open wing of the bridge, ignoring the pouring rain, while below all was complete chaos, with crewmen thrusting and shoving their way through half-naked screaming Germans, clutching their precious possessions, as if the *Varna* might sink at any moment.

'But Comrade Major,' he persisted, 'there will be a scandal – a terrible scandal! Look, Comrade.' He pointed at the port authority building. Customs men lined the rain-streaked windows. A couple of gendarmes were busy fastening on their capes at the entrance, as if they were preparing to come into the storm to investigate, while nearby a truck driver was gunning his engine furi-ously, thick blue clouds spurting from his exhaust, as if he couldn't get away from the scene of the trouble quickly enough. 'The French are already aware of what is going on – and they can board this vessel if they wish.'

Yuri, clutching the little machine pistol which he had snatched from beneath the bunk in his cabin, didn't even bother to turn to face the big worried seaman. His gaze was fixed almost hypnotically on the quayside where *they* had to emerge – if the crew didn't find them first. 'Let our vice-consul worry about that,' he snapped, feeling his nerves tingle electrically, his mind racing wildly at the thought that the whole operation was going sour... He *had* to save something of it before it was too late. 'At this moment, Captain, you'd better worry about not being sent to the Gulag.'★

'*The Gulag*!' the captain echoed fearfully. Hurriedly he crossed himself in the elaborate Russian fashion.

'*Boshe moi*,' he whispered. '*Gulag, boshe moi*!'

Yuri forgot him. His blond thatch plastered to his head by the rain, he leaned perilously out over the wing bridge, high

★ The feared Soviet prison camp system

269

above the quay. He caught a quick glimpse of the queer American who dressed in woman's clothes on the deck below. He ignored her. She played no part in what had happened, of course. She was harmless. Instead he stared along the length of deserted rain-soaked concrete, the wind lashing the raindrops into a mad dancing fury, waiting for them to appear, weapon at the ready.

Ma Barker raised her purse, one hand concealed inside it, ready for anything. Something had gone wrong, dreadfully wrong. What, she didn't know. All she knew was that there were at least three dead men on board, the SS *Varna*, and one of them was poor old Top, slaughtered by the man standing only yards away from her now. And Bluebeard had disappeared, snatched away so surprisingly and efficiently by God knows who.

For one moment she considered whether the KGB itself had a hand in it. But only for a moment. The thought was patently absurd. Why snatch him from a Russian boat when they could have sailed outside French territorial waters and done with the defector what they wished?

Yet one thing was clear in this whole mad

mess. The Russians had tumbled to Bluebeard. The little fruit with the blond hair
and his sweetie, the radio operator, wouldn't
have blown their cover otherwise. Now as
far as she was concerned, she was waiting
for her boys to get Jo-Jo out of trouble and
off the ship, and then she'd follow too, top-
speed. When the shit finally hit the fan in
Moscow, Ma Barker told herself, she didn't
want to be on the good ship *Varna*, no sir.
Now all she could do was to hold the fort
while the boys found someway, without
recoursing to violence and further scandal,
of getting themselves and the girl off the
Varna.

From below, drowning the howl of the
wind, the fury of the rain, and the panicked
cries of the elderly Germans milling the
passenger deck, came a thick, mechanical
rumbling and the clatter of rusty chains.

Yuri recognised the sound at once, if Ma
Barker didn't. 'The car deck!' he yelled at
the captain, his face wild and dripping with
rain. 'They're opening the car deck! Quick!'
He made as if to run below, but stopped just
in time as the first gleaming black Mercedes
started to trundle slowly, and obviously out
of control, down the ramp emerging from
the bowels of the SS *Varna*.

'But there's no one in it!' he yelled.

'They've just let off the brake, that's all!' the captain shrieked back, the howling wind snatching at his words. 'The owners keep the ignition keys!'

Yuri understood at once. 'Cover! They're using them as cover! He leaned out dangerously, machine pistol at the ready, eyes fixed on the ramp as the Mercedes rumbled to a stop, front wheels jammed against a bollard. Behind it, a bright green BMW sports car was lumbering down the ramp now.

'There they are!' he cried to no one in particular, and slipped his finger around the trigger of the pistol.

Suddenly several things happened at once. Over at the port authority building, the driver of the truck pressed his foot down hard on the accelerator. The big vehicle shot forward towards the *Varna*, water hosing to the rear in a furious white wake. Tiny figures, lugging what looked like a drum, bolted from behind the green BMW, which was bundling to an awkward stop. At the entrance of the port authority building the cops began to shrill their whistles urgently, fumbling for their automatics.

Yuri lost control of himself. Hardly

272

realising that he was doing so, he pressed the trigger. The little MP chattered into frenetic life at his hip.

'*Nyet*!" the captain screamed. '*Nyet, tovaritsch*!'

Mallory ducked instinctively as Robson skidded the truck round in a wild, shaking curve. A line of slugs slapped along the quay, yellow flame and sprays of concrete spurting up frighteningly. Over at the port authority building, a customs man screamed shrilly as his chest was ripped apart by a hail of ricocheting bullets, and he slammed down on the cobbles, dead.

'*For Chrissake run*!' Mallory gasped. Now Robson was roaring towards them and Mallory knew instinctively what he would do. He would swing the great truck round to shelter them from the ship. But they would have to reach it first. 'Double!' he urged fervently. '*Come on, chaps*!'

They staggered forward through the hissing rain, the wind lashing their black, soaked clothes against their limbs, bodies tensed for the hot, lethal impact of lead. Now Robson was only fifty yards away, and the running, gasping men could see the white blur of his face behind the sweep of the windscreen wipers, tense and very intent.

Behind them there was that dread crackle once more. Slugs howled off the cobbles, striking angry blue sparks. There was a sound of rending metal, then a hollow boom. Bahadur almost lost his grip as the drum shivered alarmingly in his hand. Desperately they ran on. Only thirty yards to go now.

Madly Yuri fumbled to fit a new magazine, while the captain raged behind him, soaked by the driving rain. Yuri took no notice. He was animated by a burning, unreasoning rage. He had to kill those running men down there. *He had to!*

'For God's sake, man,' a voice floated up from below as he completed the fitting and leaned out once more. 'Stop it... What do you think–' Ma Barker never completed the words. The mad light that burned in the Russian's eyes made all talk useless. At this moment the KGB man was beyond any human restraint. Ma Barker's hand jerked the little pearl-handled pistol from her purse.

Yuri was quicker. Instinctively he pressed the trigger. Ma Barker gave a shrill scream, powdered face contorted with sudden agony. At her chest the inflated bra cups exploded one after the other. Great flurries of blood were flung out by the explosion of those artificial breasts, and suddenly the front of Ma Barker's dress was flushed a bright scarlet and she was sinking weakly to the deck. Ma Barker, graduate of the US Military Academy, winner of the Silver Star for bravery in combat, had died in action.

Below, the big truck skidded to a shuddering, violent stop. In a minute the running men lugging the drum would be behind it. Desperately, his face lashed by the furious rain, Yuri fired. The driver's face disappeared behind a gleaming spider's web of glass. There was the hollow boom of metal striking metal. Slugs howled everywhere – and then they were gone, and his magazine was empty once more.

The truck roared. It swung round in a crazy circle. A man could be seen furiously fighting to get in. A brown-faced figure leaned out dangerously as the truck careened about and hauled him up. Next moment it had shot away, scattering the running gendarmes to left and right, swaying madly, little red blotches splattering the concrete behind it. A minute later it was out in the street, belting down the road at sixty miles an hour, the driving rain swallowing it up for good.

Wordlessly Yuri let the useless machine pistol clatter down to the deck. His shoulders heaved. He let his head fall to the rail. He had failed. The whole great plot had ended in total failure. Silently, like a heartbroken child, knowing that his career was over, he began to sob. Down below, the rain pelted on, turning the little blobs of bright-red blood slowly pink, until finally they vanished altogether as if they had never been there...

ENVOI

'My experience is that the gentlemen who are the best behaved and the most sleek are those who are doing the mischief. We cannot be too sure of anybody.'

Lord Ironside, June 1940

'Of course, it was a set-up right from the very start – for our cousins across the sea, as dear old Winnie used to call them. I should have guessed.' C gave Mallory one of those polite, wan smiles of his. 'You understand, Mallory, naturally?'

'Yes, sir,' Mallory said – though, of course, he didn't. C seemed greyer than ever. Perhaps it was some trick of the weak September sunshine drifting in dustily through the leaded window of the manor house, but it seemed almost as if there was a patina of grey dust on C's thin, grey hair. Mallory wasn't a particularly imaginative man, but at that moment he had the sensation that C was already dead and was slowly beginning to crumble into dust.

Outside on the well-kept lawn, the men of Alpha Team were drinking beer out of cans and eating slices of cold pizza brought from Stroud. C glanced at the bronzed young men idly and said, 'I suppose your chaps are accustomed to that sort of food, Mallory. Terrible, what?'

'Yes, sir,' Mallory replied dutifully.

'With hindsight, naturally, we should have realised it even then. It was all too easy. A colonel of the KGB, high in the hierarchy of Directorate 5, being allowed to defect – just like that.' He clicked his fingers together, and Mallory noted his annoyance. 'Handed to the Americans on a silver platter. Not on.' He shook his head in mild disapproval. 'Thank goodness, we pranged the whole op.' He tut-tutted hastily. 'There I go again with that silly slang of mine. *Pranged* indeed!'

Opposite the old man at the big oak table, surrounded by the mementos of three centuries of service to the Crown – ragged battle flags, yellowing photographs of bewhiskered generals, cases of tarnished and fading medals – Mallory found himself frowning in bewilderment. 'Do you mean, sir, that Bluebeard wasn't what he seemed to be?'

'Exactly.'

Outside, Ross was throwing pieces of pizza to the swans in the ornamental pond. But being the kind of upper-class swans they were, they refused to pick up the dough in tall-necked, aloof disdain. In the end Ross gave up and, red-faced with anger as usual, gave them the two fingers.

'But what was the object of the whole business then, sir?' Mallory asked, once more feeling himself being caught up in the slimy morass of the Intelligence world.

'Two things, I suppose.' C held up a claw-like finger. 'One, to compromise us, as you know, by revealing to the Americans the Soviet moles in our service. Two, Bluebeard would then sacrifice some of Directorate S's lesser agents. This would get him into the good graces of the CIA and they would then undoubtedly have recruited him as a high-level consultant for their own services. They always do. Take Frolik, for example. Why should they ever have suspected him?' He shrugged his skinny shoulders. 'After all, he was – er, naming names.' He grinned faintly at Mallory at his choice of expression. 'Do you think I'm improving? Getting *with it*, as they say, Mallory?'

'Undoubtedly, sir,' Mallory said hastily, hoping to divert C's attention from the fact that outside, Robson, slightly drunk on the beer, was zipping open his flies to urinate in a hot stream on C's prize roses.

'What a feather in the cap of the KGB it would have been! Their own man right in the heart of Langley, spreading hate between two allies, and at the same time neatly transmitting vital information about the working of the CIA back to Moscow. Philby in his heyday couldn't have done better!'

There was a moment or two's heavy silence. Outside, Robson, flies done up again and obviously more drunk than Mallory had suspected, was singing lustily, *'Now this is number one and I've got her on the run. Roll me over, lay me down and do it again! Roll me over ... in the clover... Roll me, lay me down and do it again...'*

C smiled wanly. 'How good it is to hear the brave songs of one's remote youth,' he said obscurely, and sighed. 'Naturally we came out of the whole sordid affair smelling of attar of roses, Mallory,' he continued. 'The Americans are tremendously impressed by our acumen and efficiency. They think we conducted the whole op to save them from themselves now.'

'And the moles, sir? The ones Bluebeard was going to tell them about?'

'All forgotten now, my dear boy. We've kissed and made up. It's honeymoon time in London once more. After all, the two main chaps involved, that Sergeants' Mess type and the one who, er,' C frowned slightly, 'dressed up as a woman are now deceased.' He chuckled at some thought of his own.

'The moles have been conveniently dismissed. In due course, we shall take care of them ourselves. Discreetly, naturally. One of them used to be a member of parliament, we hear. Only a Liberal one, though. Fortunately. Nobody much cares what Liberals do or don't do, what?' Again, he chuckled. 'So there we are. The whole op has been a success in failure, if I may phrase it that way. Good work, Mallory. In due course there will be a discreet gong in it for you and your chaps, but not just yet, while the heat, as I think they say these days, is on. Not yet.'

He let his words sink in and waited for a reaction from Mallory, but none came. The thought of the 'discreet gong' didn't thrill him; it left him numb, just as he had been numb since that terrible discovery on the rainsoaked parking lot off the *route nationale* that led from Orange to Lyons that Bluebeard was dead. Dead – slumped in a pool of his own blood at the bottom of the drum, his back ripped apart by that last burst of gunfire from the SS *Varna*. Mallory recalled how he had looked down at that moonlike face, contorted by agony, and thought how he must have suffered, dying alone and trapped in the back of the truck as it continued racing north. At that moment he had felt a sense of loss and numbness the like of which he had never experienced before. Everything – all the effort, the work, the danger – had been for this: a helpless man, Communist spymaster though he was, dying in the rumbling, trembling blackness of the truck, without even a single other human being to hear his last words.

'Naturally, you and your chaps will have to drop out of sight for a little while,' C continued, and now the deceptive softness had vanished from his voice. Mallory's numbness disappeared suddenly. There was something in the air. He could almost smell it.

'Drop out of sight, sir?' he echoed, urging C mentally to get on with it.

'Yes. How would you like a long holiday in South America, for example?'

'Argentina, sir?' Mallory asked eagerly.

'No, no. Not the Falklands business again, my dear boy.' C gave him one of those secret smiles of his. 'This is connected with an older war, a much older one, indeed, one fought before you were born, in fact.'

'You mean World War Two, sir?'

'Exactly.'

'But that's over forty years ago now, sir.

And anyway, what's South America got to do with it? The South Americans, or most of them, didn't even fight in that war....'

Mallory's voice died away as C held up his grey, clawlike hand for silence. 'Let me tell you a tale, Mallory, a tale of treachery, and money bought with innocent blood, and an officer who betrayed not only his country but his own comrades. Let me tell you the tale of Operation Vermin...'

Mallory settled back. Even before C had commenced his story, he knew that Alpha Team, the Special Boat Service, was going on ops again...

The publishers hope that this book has given you enjoyable reading. Large Print Books are especially designed to be as easy to see and hold as possible. If you wish a complete list of our books please ask at your local library or write directly to:

Magna Large Print Books
Magna House, Long Preston,
Skipton, North Yorkshire.
BD23 4ND

This Large Print Book, for people
who cannot read normal print,
is published under the auspices of

THE ULVERSCROFT FOUNDATION

... we hope you have enjoyed this book.
Please think for a moment about those
who have worse eyesight than you ...
and are unable to even read or enjoy
Large Print without great difficulty.

You can help them by sending a
donation, large or small, to:

**The Ulverscroft Foundation,
1, The Green, Bradgate Road,
Anstey, Leicestershire, LE7 7FU,
England.**
or request a copy of our brochure for
more details.

The Foundation will use all donations
to assist those people who are visually
impaired and need special attention
with medical research, diagnosis
and treatment.

Thank you very much for your help.